GW00535756

THE WARRIOR RETREAT

JOHN LYNCH

Copyright © 2022 by John Lynch

All rights reserved.

Edited by Patrick C. Harrison III

Cover by Michael Squid

No part of this book may be reproduced in any form or by any electronic or mechanical means, including information storage and retrieval systems, without written permission from the author, except for the use of brief quotations in a book review.

To Britney, Ava, William, and Ronan.

Come on, you sons of bitches-do you want to live forever?

GUNNERY SERGEANT DAN DALY,
USMC, JUNE 1918

PART ONE
THE WAR ABROAD

ONE
A NOCTURNAL VISIT

Something ripped Ray from his slumber, long before his alarm was due to go off. Even before he realized he couldn't move, a feeling of dread grew in his stomach, like he had swallowed a large stone. Eyes wide open, he stared at the underside of Paul's bunk. The oppressive heat alone was bad enough, but waking up paralyzed was enough to fuck up anyone's day. Even now, in July, the hottest month of the Iraqi summer, the heat was poised to reach record heights. The temperature outside of his room had not dropped below 90 degrees, even though the sun had set hours ago. With no air conditioning or ventilation to speak of, the metal trailer used as a dwelling was likely as hot, if not hotter, than the sweltering Iraqi climate outside. Despite the heat, he shivered, goosebumps trailing along his arm. Something was triggering his body's fight-or-flight response while also rendering him unable to do either of those things. Clenching his teeth, Ray strained, struggling to move his body.

He failed.

No longer afforded the luxury of locomotion, Ray swiveled his eyeballs in their sockets. That small motion at least was still within his grasp. He scanned for either of his two room-mates, hoping that one of them could help. Passed out on a beanbag chair in the center of the room, was his buddy, Mark. Paul tossed and turned on the bunk above him. Whatever malady left Ray in his current vegetative state had skipped Paul, and possibly Mark. Although Ray supposed that until Mark woke up, there was no way to know for sure. During their downtime, and in an effort to wind down and disconnect from the always on alert, patrol mindset, the three Marines had spent the past few weeks binge-watching the entire series run of *Buffy the Vampire Slayer* on DVD. During the night, the three of them had all fallen asleep without turning off either the television, or the DVD player. Still playing on the old CRT set was Ray's favorite episode, "Once more with feeling." He loved how the entire episode was done as a musical; it was genius. That the disc was still playing an episode and had not yet reverted to the main menu told Ray that he couldn't have been asleep for very long. Only an hour or two. Tops.

Sweat trickled down his spine, running along the crack of his ass before pooling on the mattress beneath him. The air inside the room changed. What the cause of the change could be, Ray did not know. The air became dense, and not from the smothering heat, but different. It took on an almost crushing weight, transforming the simple, involuntary task of breathing into a life and death struggle.

The hairs on his neck stood alert, and Ray's testicles felt as if they had ascended back into his body, nestling in the pit of his stomach. He had the distinct feeling he was being watched. It reminded him of sitting in front of the television as a child playing video games. His brother, Mike, would try to sneak up on him, and although Mike hadn't made a peep, Ray *felt* his presence behind him.

With the memory of that feeling fresh in his mind, Ray struggled with a newfound urgency, again failing to move.

Ray refused to give up. Figuring this shit out was imperative. He was certain his life depended on it.

Staring at his feet, he focused on his toes. Maybe if he could regain control of some small part of his body, he could reclaim the rest.

Did I have a stroke? A seizure? What the fuck is going on?

It was no use. Ray was a fucking cripple, his massive frame as useless as a limp dick in a threesome. He needed to wake one of his roommates so they could call for the platoon's Navy Corpsman. He opened his mouth to speak, but the words wouldn't come.

Between his legs, a swirling black vortex formed on the mattress.

From the vortex, something rose. Inch by inch, the thing emerged from the mattress. As it continued to take shape, the black, amorphous *thing* took on physical traits. Before long, he was staring at a woman's head.

Ray's heart jackhammered in his chest, threatening to burst at any second, leaving him dead. He wouldn't even be given the honor of dying in combat. Maybe a heart attack was a better fate than living the rest of his life as a vegetable, or worse, living long enough to discover whatever the fuck was going on between his legs.

He was losing his mind. That had to be it. The pressure of combat—always wondering when you were going to be sniped, blown up by an IED, or taken out by some chicken shit with a bomb strapped to his chest—had finally cracked his mind, leaving him a few eggs short of a full basket.

Behind a veil of long, black hair, the apparition stared at

him. Black eyes set above high cheekbones. Her skin pale with death and her body covered in dirt from the grave.

Terror gripped him, and Ray once again tried to scream, but his vocal cords did not cooperate. A wet warmth spread forth from his crotch. The stench of rotting flesh commingled with his own piss, assaulting his nostrils and turning his stomach sour. The specter, now fully materialized and kneeling on his chest, grabbed at his neck with her long, dirty fingers. Each one of its fingernails felt sharp enough to easily slice through flesh like a knife through warm butter.

Ray stared in horror as she grinned, revealing a mouthful of decaying and broken teeth, set in a charred and blackened face. The phantom's skin was cracked in places, much like hardened, broken clay. Entire sections of skin were missing, revealing the muscle and bone behind it. Ray could see a few of her molars through the rot in her skin.

She really should brush her teeth better. Yep, his mind had cracked alright.

The grisly ghoul had an air of familiarity about her, and it sparked Ray's memory. He had seen this woman before and had played a role in her death.

She had been the victim of collateral damage from a mortar strike on an enemy compound. Ray was the squad leader, but the off-target round wasn't his fault. The unit's forward observer had called in the request for fire, and his squad had dropped the rounds on the coordinates provided to them. Mortar systems are indirect fire weapons which by nature meant that it was impossible for him to see his target. Your aim could be perfect, but if the observer was wrong, or the mathematics involved in converting the forward observer's surveillance into mils on a compass were wrong, the round would not go where intended.

Still struggling underneath the weight of the corpse, tears

trickled down his cheeks. He felt awful about what happened. He would never intentionally harm a civilian, and her death weighed heavily upon his conscience. The night it had happened he had even considered suicide, unsure how he could live the rest of his life knowing that he was a responsible for the death of a non-combatant. Sure, he had taken lives before, but they had all been enemy combatants. Never a woman who had simply been in the wrong place at the wrong time.

She tightened her grip around his neck and pressed her lips against his. The tendons in his neck strained, bulging like ripcords, ready to split the thin layer of skin over them. The specter lost shape, deflating like a balloon losing helium. Now a shapeless mass, she forced her way through Ray's mouth, stifling his last attempt to scream.

Ray's body convulsed. His bowels emptied and shit blossomed out of his asshole, the force of the evacuation splattering the brown, watery mess along his ass cheeks and the back of his thighs.

A set of arms grabbed him by the shoulders, pinning him down.

"Dude, snap the fuck out of it," Paul said. "Did you just fucking shit yourself?"

"What? What's going on?" Ray asked.

"You had another nightmare. You were shaking the shit out of my bunk. I climbed down and you were spazzing the fuck out."

"I can't sleep, man. And when I do, I keep seeing everyone we've killed. I need to talk to Doc. Get some sleeping pills or something," Ray said.

"You need to let that shit go, man, we're in a war. Accidents happen. It wasn't your fault."

"Yeah… yeah I know."

Paul scratched his nuts. "Get in the shower and clean yourself up. It fucking stinks in here, and I'm not cleaning this shit up. After that, go see Doc, because we need your head in the game."

Both Marines let the conversation die there.

After cleaning himself and the room, Ray tossed his sheets in the trash and threw a poncho liner on his bunk. Laying on the bunk, Ray wondered what was wrong with him.

He could not sleep, while Paul had fallen back to sleep almost instantly, and Mark had somehow remained asleep for the entirety of what had happened, completely unaware of anything that had transpired.

TWO
QRF UP!

T he sun rose overhead, making good on the promise of super-heating Camp Fallujah. Ray rolled out of his bunk and put his uniform on. He picked up his hygiene kit and stepped outside, cursing the already oppressive heat. The air threatened to cook his eyeballs. It reminded him of opening an oven with your face too close to the door. He took a deep breath, choking on the fumes of flaming human shit. Every morning some poor soul had to stir a concoction of JP-8 and human feces. A foul mixture that ruined the urge to eat breakfast every day since Ray had been in country. He thanked God every morning that he had the foresight to fake a respiratory illness, exempting him from shit burning duty. Hell, knowing how bad that detail was, Ray figured he owed the doc a blowjob for exempting him.

Despite being in the middle of a war zone that stunk of death, decay, and human shit, the mornings in Iraq were peaceful, and sticking to a morning hygiene routine allowed Ray to hold on to a shred of normalcy, one that had kept him sane. Until last night.

Today, as he brushed his teeth, Ray did not feel sane. His

mind played last night's nightmare on a loop. Ray told himself that it had been nothing more than a vivid dream, but there was a part of him that didn't believe it. Those dead eyes. They peered into the depths of his soul. Ray thought of how she violated his body. No, that was no dream. He had taken an innocent life, and now he would pay.

He vomited, spraying the foul contents of his stomach against the side of the trailer and in the dirt at his feet. It got on his boots and coated his uniform pants.

After the violent expulsion of what little food had been in his stomach, Ray tried to compose himself. He rubbed his eyes. The bags under his eyes had bags. He needed to sleep, but his body refused to cooperate. His squad had finished their turn on patrol and were now on rest, but they remained on Quick React Force duty. QRF was a mixed bag. There would be no scheduled missions, but being assigned QRF meant you needed to be ready to leave the wire at a moment's notice. Any rest a Marine on QRF got could be interrupted at a moment's notice. Emergency response was needed on an almost daily basis.

In order to accommodate the need for haste, the QRF team left their gear staged in the trucks according to their respective vehicle assignments. Ray was the driver of the lead vehicle, one of the most important assignments on any patrol, and after his morning hygiene was complete, the next part of his routine was a maintenance check of his vehicle. He felt out of focus, and tried to force his mind to clear the cobwebs, but the fog enveloping his brain remained. This was more than the usual morning grogginess. He pulled a can of Red Bull from his assault pack, cracked the tab and chugged it in one go. If he was lucky, the liquid energy boost would pump a few more hours of life into his walking corpse.

After sucking down the canned coronary, Ray grabbed his

shaving kit, ready to finish his morning hygiene. He splashed water on his face and neck. Ray hated shaving, and wished he could stop. Plenty of guys could go a day or two without shaving, but no, not him. He had to be one of those hairy, sasquatch mother fuckers who had a five o'clock shadow five minutes after he put the razor down. Even in the middle of a war, Marines were required to maintain grooming standards. Some fuckwad in command that never left his tent, never had to see the horrors of war, decided that the insurgents gave a fuck if you shaved or not, and that they would assume an unshaven Marine was an unprepared Marine. You couldn't make up something that fucking stupid. Ray laughed at the absurdity of the thought. It was bullshit, but so was 90% of the shit the Marine Corps force-fed their enlistees. It was a method of indoctrination, and the Marines had developed plenty of those over the past 200-plus years of its existence.

Ray set his mirror down on the electrical box outside of his room, placing it at an angle allowing him to see his face. He grabbed his can of Barbasol and shook it, pressing the button and pumping a large puff of white foam into his hands. He worked it into a lather, raised his hands to his face, and stopped dead in his tracks.

Bruises lined his neck.

Bruises that looked like hands.

He stared, mouth agape. Ray didn't know if the rigors of war were chipping away at his mind, or if the ghost of a woman who had died a horrible death at his hands had returned for revenge. Either way, it didn't matter. Both of the options fucking terrified him.

He closed his eyes and shook his head. When he opened them, the marks were gone.

He wasn't *losing* his mind; it was long fucking gone.

Radio chatter from his hip ripped him from his trance,

forcing him back to reality. Mark and Paul burst out of their room carrying their weapons.

"Let's go, Fucker! Second platoon got hit! We're up!" Paul called over his shoulder.

Ray left his hygiene kit where it lay. There was no time to clean up. Face still lathered, he snatched his rifle off the ground and sprinted toward the trucks, leaving a trail of Barbasol in his wake.

THREE
ONE HELL OF A BLAST

S itting in the driver seat, foot on the pedal, Ray led the convoy down the main supply route. The promotion to lead driver was something that Ray had welcomed with open arms, despite the responsibility of finding a clear path over roads that could be, and usually were, littered with explosives. Despite the daunting responsibility, he much preferred his current position to his previous billet of rear vehicle driver. That position came with two major issues. The first being the vehicle itself. The rear vehicle was a flat-bed truck with little armor, no gun turret, and a floorboard that had rotted so badly that you could see the ground beneath the truck. The truck had no business bringing up the rear, but unfortunately their patrol commander didn't utilize common sense when organizing patrols. There was something truly unnerving about looking down at the gas pedal, seeing the white lines or dirt road beneath you, knowing that at any moment an IED could explode beneath you. Ray supposed if there was a saving grace to that truck, it was that if you *were* blown up, it was guaranteed death. At least you wouldn't be permanently disabled and disfigured for the rest of your life. That small silver-lining aside, it wasn't exactly a vehicle worthy of combat operations.

The second issue, which to Ray was far worse than the likely death awaiting occupants of the previously aforementioned vehicle, was the person riding in the passenger seat, Micha Menard. Micha was the most backwater, hillbilly son-of-a-bitch he had ever met. The kid was a cunt hair over 20-years-old, but looked like a 45-year-old recovering crackhead. One would be forgiven for mistaking Micha as having played a starring role in one of the *Wrong Turn* flicks. He was about as educated as one of those inbred fucks, too.

The burst of energy that the Red Bull had gifted Ray was short-lived. He blinked rapidly, shaking his head, attempting in vain to force his body awake. It didn't matter; he was running on fumes. Despite the overwhelming exhaustion threatening to take control, he could still maintain a straight path. He guided the truck over the fractured, war-ravaged roads, maintaining a decent speed while still avoiding potholes and other potentially fatal hazards. When you drove along the same roads daily it became second nature, and you eventually learned everything about the route. New potholes, potholes that were deeper than they were the day before. Pieces of trash, or other out-of-place objects that had appeared seemingly out of nowhere. All things that to a random person meant absolutely nothing, but to an experienced combat Marine, were the signs of an IED.

Tired enough that he was practically bobbing for cock in the driver's seat, Ray somehow still kept the vehicle on a safe path. Hell, even if he missed something, there was no doubt in his mind that Lance Corporal Torres would catch the mistake and alert him to it well before it became a problem.

That kid had eyes like a fucking hawk. If there was something in the road, Torres would spot it. Or so Ray hoped.

Ray looked to the passenger on his right, the patrol commander, Sergeant Stevens. "Do we have any more Rip Its, Sergeant?"

"Why? Is Paul keeping you up all night, Devil Dog?"

Ray shook his head. Despite being in a war zone that reached temperatures hotter than Satan's shit factory, the worst part of day-to-day life overseas was interacting with Stevens. The guy never knew when to shut the fuck up. He regularly offended everyone around him and was a dumbass. To make matters worse, the man was so universally loathed in his own company that more than one of his fellow brothers-in-arms were known to be laying the pipe to his wife. They didn't even bother attempting to hide it, and he did not put a stop to it. It was impossible to let your wife cuck you, and somehow expect that a group of type A, war-fighting men would have even a shred of respect for you. Then again, Stevens wasn't the type to earn his respect, he was the type to shout about his rank and demand respect, while perpetually doing everything in his power to make sure that he never actually earned it. Men like Stevens were the reason people thought Marines to be stupid, crayon-eating, testosterone-fueled fuckwads. Except he didn't even fit the musclebound stereotype; he was nothing more than a moron. Anyone who wondered why people joked about the Crayola inspired culinary habits of a United States Marine needn't look any further than Stevens.

Ray smiled as Marcus Simpson laughed from the back seat of the vehicle. "I got you, Ray. I stole an entire case from behind Captain America's hooch last night." He passed the tiny 8 ounce can of liquid crack to Ray.

"Not the first little thing you held in your hand this morning, is it, Huggies?" Stevens asked Ray.

"Real fucking original, Sergeant," Ray said. On Ray's first day with his unit, Stevens mispronounced his last name, Hughes, as Huggies. Stevens, not wanting to sound like a moron, played it off as a joke. Those who laughed were not laughing at Ray, they were laughing at what an assclown Stevens was. Of course, the imbecile was none the wiser. Thinking his fake joke had landed with the audience, the name stuck and Ray would be known as Huggies forevermore.

Ray cracked the can open, finishing the entirety in one long sip. He tossed the aluminum container out the window. He knew it was wrong. *Trash is everywhere*, he told himself. If the citizens didn't care to keep it clean, why should he? When he first landed in the country, he would have never done such a thing, and certainly wouldn't have harbored those thoughts, but war changes people. It brings out the absolute worst in even the best men and women. And as he desensitized himself toward the loss of human life, he found it even easier to disassociate the country with the rest of the planet.

Stevens once again interrupted the vehicle's blissful silence. "Ray, let me ask you this. I've been hitting the gym, getting my swoll on, but I'm having trouble packing on muscle. I mean, my love muscle is fine, but my pecs. I'm trying to turn my man tits into pecs. I think I'm jacking off too much, do you lose testosterone from jacking off?"

"What the fuck? Is that a serious question?" Ray took his eyes off the road and stared at Stevens. He couldn't tell if Stevens was busting his balls or if the man really was that stupid. Knowing Stevens, it wasn't beyond the realm of possibility that, yes, he really was that fucking stupid. "Man, cut this shit. You can't be that dumb." Normally, Ray wouldn't speak to a sergeant in that manner, but the lack of sleep and the onslaught of day in and day out jackassery had pushed him over that line. If Stevens wanted to make an issue of the disrespect, Ray would gladly deal with the reper-cussions.

Stevens glared at Ray for a moment. The look on his face spoke the words that surely must be running through his mind. "First off," Stevens said, "Watch how you fucking talk to me. You would do well to remember your rank, and that both my rank and billet exceed what you will ever achieve in the Marine Corps, doubly so, considering I do your fucking proficiency and conduct reports, Marine."

Ray inhaled, but kept his cool hoping he could smooth this one over and avoid facing discipline.

Stevens quickly reverted to his normal self, punching Ray in the shoulder. The punch to the arm was further proof of Stevens inability to take anything serious. The man didn't even have the common sense to not fuck with the man trying to focus on potential roadside hazards, and showed ignorance to the fact that causing Ray to swerve off his route could be fatal to everyone in the truck. "I'm just busting your balls, Huggies. But seriously, is that a no? There's no harm in beating my meat?"

Ray slowly exhaled the breath that he had been holding, it had done little to calm his nerves. "You can do whatever you want, Sergeant," Ray said.

From the back of the truck, Marcus called out, "Stevens, you really are a fucking dumbass, you know that?"

"Watch it, Lance Corporal," Stevens replied.

Ray rolled his eyes. If Stevens would do nothing about *his* talking out of turn, he sure as shit would not do a damn thing about Marcus. Not that Ray was a pussy, and he *was* physically imposing, but Stevens had no backbone, and if today *was* the day that Stevens reached down and found a set of nuts in that fleshy patch between his legs, he was liable to have a near death experience. You didn't fuck with Simpson. You could hide behind your rank in garrison, but overseas, anyone and everyone was available to catch hands. Marcus was a bad motherfucker. The only man in the squad who matched Ray in size. But where Ray was laid back and reserved, Simpson would beat you within an inch of your life at the slightest transgression. You didn't want to piss him off.

Back in Hawaii, on their last free weekend before the deployment was scheduled to kick off, a few dozen Weapons Company Marines started what they intended as the first of a series of bi-annual pub crawls. One last hurrah before they went boots on the ground overseas, facing what they were told would be certain death. The second of the bi-annual pub crawls was reserved for those lucky enough to not have gotten their ticket to hell punched. It was grim, but most of the guys had dark humor, and even more genuinely expected to die.

More to the point, the pub crawls were simply another excuse to get shit-faced in Waikiki.

The night had started off like any other weekend, except this time they were rolling deep to the bars. Depending on how you looked at that, it could be perceived as either a good or bad situation. On the bad hand, you had a few dozen drunk Marines causing a ruckus. On the good hand, it would be damn near impossible that one of them would get jumped by the locals, which happened more often than any of them liked to admit.

The safety in numbers had worked out well until Marcus had gotten separated from the rest of the group. The night had been well underway, and everyone had had far too many drinks, rendering it impossible to keep tabs on one another. By the time anyone had noticed Marcus was missing, the sun had been up for hours and most of the guys were indulging in whatever hangover cure they swore by.

At some point, Marcus had returned to base, but nobody knew when exactly. He had simply arrived, as if he materialized out of thin air. But that was the Simpson way; it wasn't the first time, nor would it be the last.

When everyone had gathered in the common area to piece together all the missing fragments of the night, Marcus kicked open the swinging door, alive and well, but missing a single shoe. Blood and filth covered his sock. When asked about it, he responded, "I was walking in an alleyway, and some tough guy had a problem with the color of my skin. I stomped his head into the ground. I think I killed a man, but I didn't stick around to find out. If he's alive, he ain't happy."

And that was the thing about Marcus Simpson—stories like that were a dime a dozen, but most of them lacked witnesses to corroborate them. There was no way to filter fact from fiction. Either way, nobody would put it past him; they'd all seen what he could do. They'd all seen Simpson take his pound of flesh, and none of them, Ray included, were about to call him out for telling tall tales.

The convoy continued along the route for what felt like an eternity, the only break in the monotony, the endless heckling of one another. Even during an emergency response, the banter never stopped. They busted each other's balls in a way that most outside the military could never understand.

Something hit the back of Ray's helmet hard enough that his head almost whacked the steering wheel.

"What the fuck?" Ray said.

"You're bobbing for cock again, dumbass. You fall asleep

again and you're going to be explaining that to the First Serg…"

Stevens never finished his sentence.

A gigantic blast rocked the truck. The noise was deafening. Rock and dirt exploded outward, while shrapnel punched through the armor of Ray's vehicle. Dozens of shards of metal, all capable of killing a man, along with hundreds of ball bearings, screws, and nails flew around the truck. Flesh and bone were penetrated, ripped apart. Blood splattered in the truck, painting faces and uniforms with a fine red mist.

* * *

The concussive blast brought the truck to an immediate halt, propelling Marcus forward, into the empty seat directly in front of him. The combination of a well-padded seat and body armor helped to cushion the impact against his body, but could not stop his head from slamming against the window, striking it first with his Kevlar helmet, followed by his face, his nose crunching against the glass, flattening it and sending blood spraying forth.

"Fuck," he shouted as the impact continued to ping-pong him around the truck.

He picked himself up from the floor of the truck and scanned his surroundings. From what he could tell, the IED had been a big one, and new, too. The MRAP they rode in, which was the latest combat truck utilized by the Marine Corps, had armor specifically designed for maximum safety in this kind of attack. Every time the coalition made advances in IED defense, it wasn't long before the insurgency figured out a way around them. The enemy was far more intelligent than anyone who wasn't on the front lines would give them credit for.

"You guys ok?" Simpson asked.

No response from anyone in the truck. *Fuck, I hope it's not too bad.*

Simpson looked up, checking for Torres. The small hammock used as a gunner seat was empty. The only sign that Torres had been there previously was the large amount of blood saturating the material of the seat, dripping down to the vehicle floor where it pooled and spread.

So much for hoping things weren't too bad.

Looking around the area surrounding the growing pool of blood, Simpson's eyes found Torres.

Or rather, what was left of him?

Resting against the rear passenger-side door was a severed leg. Scraps of tattered, bloody uniform fused with the bloody hunk of meat. Shards of bone were visible both sticking out from the stump, and through the areas where jagged shards of metal had torn through the flesh at high velocity, ripping and tearing through flesh, muscle, and bone alike.

Marcus leaned forward over the metal table bolted to the floor between the front driver and passenger-side seats. Through the smoke and dust, it was impossible to see either Ray or Stevens. Marcus called out again, expecting—and receiving—no response in return. Marcus's massive frame—along with the claustrophobic close quarters of the MRAP—made getting to the front seat impossible. He squeezed an arm past the table and into the seating area, and after much difficulty feeling around, located both Stevens and Hughes. With his vision completely obscured, and the bulk of both of their protective gear, Marcus could not determine if the men were unconscious or dead. He hoped for the former, but expected the latter.

With Ray and Stevens both out of the equation, and

Torres either dead or horribly maimed, but at the present missing, Simpson knew he needed to act hastily, and with surgical precision. Foremost, he needed to call in a nine-line casualty evacuation. Not knowing the extent of the damage, he would assume the worst in order to get the helo in the air and support en route.

Once again, Simpson squeezed what little of his body he could through the space between the front seats, grasping for Stevens radio. He gritted his teeth, stretching as far as he could. His pectoral and shoulder muscles strained as they reached the limit of his body's flexibility. Simpson was about to give up when his fingers grazed the cord, knocking the radio slightly closer.

He continued to stretch, at last getting a three-fingered grip on the radio. Bringing the small black box to his mouth, Simpson willed his body to focus on what they had drilled into them daily for the last eight months. Remain calm, get the bird in the air.

Simpson keyed the radio. "Whiskey Actual, this is Whiskey QRF. Standby for nine line cas-evac. Over."

A burst of static, followed by a voice on the other end, "Whiskey One, this is Whiskey Actual. I read you Lima Charlie. Send it."

The full report was nine lines. In order to get a bird in the air for evacuation, five were immediately necessary, the other four could follow with help en route. Simpson keyed the mic, clearly delivering those five vital lines.

Line one: Location
Line two: Call Sign and frequency
Line three: Number of casualties by precedence
Line four: Special Equipment required
Line five: Number of patients by type

Simpson delivered the required information clearly and

concisely. Seeing no moving bodies, he assumed that all three casualties would require a litter.

The Marine on the other end of the radio broke the silence. "Roger that, Whiskey One, solid copy. We have a bird enroute. Over."

Simpson exhaled. With the most important part of the nine lines out of the way, he could reassess the current situation and determine a course of action. The chatter on local coms—in coordination with the background gunfire—told him that the rest of his squad was currently engaged with the enemy. He needed to do what he could for the casualties and get to the fight. Before exiting the truck, he needed to give a few more lines of the nine line, at least enough to let the chopper know they were flying in on a hot LZ.

Simpson grabbed the radio and relayed the rest of the evacuation report. The voice on the other end received the info, and Simpson broke communication. It was time to get some. Simpson opened the rear door, checking at his feet for secondary IEDs. After doing a visual sweep, and now confident there were no other devices immediately in front of him, Simpson hopped out of the back door, hugging close to the vehicle with his weapon at the ready, and continued around the passenger side of the vehicle, watching for both IEDs in his direct path, and enemy combatants in the distance.

After swiftly and methodically making his way to the passenger door, Simpson yanked it open. The heavy door resisted initially, but once it moved, momentum swung it forward. Stevens' lifeless body slid out of the open doorway, falling on Simpson. Despite his massive frame, and his freakish strength, the dead weight of Stevens and the eighty pounds of a full combat load—weapons, armor, and ammunition—proved to be too heavy for Simpson, and he fell to the ground, pinned beneath the mangled corpse of his platoon sergeant.

Blood and entrails that had once been housed inside of Stevens had been evicted from their home, and now coated Simpson in a pink and crimson, pulpy mess. Large chunks of flesh and muscle were missing, evaporated by the explosion. Fragments of bone and metal protruded from the carnage-ravaged cadaver. Simpson hoped Stevens had died on impact, that the man hadn't suffered.

Simpson turned his head, not wanting to look directly into his platoon sergeant's dead eyes. This was a different thousand-yard stare. This was the stare of the dead.

He spat blood in the dirt, not sure if the blood was his, Stevens' or a mixture of both. Probably it was both. Simpson strained, grinding his teeth as he engaged every fiber of muscle in his body. With a taxing effort, Simpson flipped Stevens' corpse off of him. If it hadn't been for the constant dump of adrenaline flooding through his system since the strike, he might not have been able to move the body.

Scrambling to his feet, Simpson took Stevens' ammo from the front of his body armor and grabbed Stevens' rifle from his battered corpse. The rifle had an M203 grenade launcher attached to it. Ray and Stevens were the only two men on the convoy equipped with the M203. Simpson didn't want that falling into enemy hands. Besides, from the sounds of the near constant gunfire, he ascertained that this firefight was going to be a hard-fought affair. A far cry from the typical hit-and-run tactics that the enemy had engaged them with up to this point. The insurgents were out to get their pound of flesh. Unfortunately for them, finding Torres' severed leg and Stevens' broken body had awakened a blood-lust within him that no bar fight in Waikiki had previously done.

"Arrggghhhh," a blood-curdling scream from somewhere in front of the truck.

Simpson ran his hand down Stevens' face, closing his eyelids. He didn't like the man, but he was still a Marine, and Simpson wanted to provide him with that last decency.

Simpson ran toward the scream, not sure what he would find. When he rounded the front of the vehicle, he spotted the source of the wails of agony. About 20 meters in front of the vehicle, Torres lay on the ground, writhing in pain, both hands clutching the stump where his leg had been. The force of the IED detonation had launched Torres from the seat in the turret, up and over the protective shield, and into the dirt road ahead of the truck. Between the missing limb, and whatever other injuries he'd received from both the blast and the ejection, Simpson thought Torres was lucky to still be alive. Or maybe it was *bad* luck, Simpson couldn't be sure. The tortured howls were something Simpson had never heard come from a grown man before, they sounded like the dying wails of some kind of animal. Seeing his friend lying there in the dirt, with his life essence pooling around him sparked a transition in Simpson's mentality, taking him from a blood-thirsty warrior to a combat lifesaver.

"Corpsman up!" Simpson yelled into his personal radio as he sprinted to Torres. He needed to act swiftly and render lifesaving aid to Torres as soon as possible—without it, he might bleed out before the corpsman responded from whatever he was doing at the moment, likely assisting another wounded Marine.

"My fucking leg man, it's gone. It's fucking gone," Torres screamed.

Simpson was speechless. What could he possibly say to comfort a man who'd just had his leg blown off. Nothing he could think of, so he decided dark humor might do the trick.

They all had sick senses of humor anyway, so it was worth the shot. "Nah man, you've still got maybe a quarter of it. A little more if you count that bone sticking out."

Torres laughed despite the pain

"Just give me the drugs, man. This shit hurts like a motherfucker," Torres said.

"Ok," Simpson said. "First we put the tourniquet on that stump, then we get the morphine and party."

Typically, only the Navy Corpsman attached to a Marine patrol was issued morphine, but there had been a heavy uptick in casualties recently, and Battalion Command had authorized all individual Marines to carry morphine auto injectors. Issuing such a drug to young men was a horrible idea, but the deployment had been a nightmare and desperate times called for desperate measures.

Simpson got to work on Torres' leg. *If they have to cut below this tourniquet, he will have nowhere close to a quarter of his leg left*, he thought. He tied the tourniquet off, cinching it as tight as possible. Torres let out a sharp breath, but Simpson wasn't too concerned about hurting him with the tourniquet, if he didn't stop this bleeding, Torres would have bigger problems.

With the tourniquet in place and blood no longer gushing, Simpson ran his hands along Torres' body, searching for other signs of hemorrhaging. Miraculously, there were no other major injuries to speak of aside from the leg. Maybe some broken bones, but Simpson couldn't be sure. Simpson couldn't believe it. "You're one lucky fucker, Torres."

"Yeah? I don't feel so lucky."

"No, I guess you probably don't. The good news is you're about to not feel much of anything." As Simpson rummaged through Torres' first aid kit, gunfire erupted yet again and bullets struck the dirt in front of him, too close for comfort.

"Hold on," Simpson said, grabbing the strap on Torres' body armor and dragging him across the dirt, back to the side of the truck. He should have done it as soon as he'd gotten the tourniquet on, but when bullets are flying and men are bleeding out, it's difficult to make the right call at the drop of a dime.

Simpson searched the aid pouch again, finding the morphine syrette. He knew Doc should be the one to determine morphine use. It was a no go if head injuries were involved, and they'd just been in an IED blast and it didn't take a rocket scientist to surmise Torres had probably gotten his bell rung. That being said, his brother in arms was in pain, and probably could very well die. If that happened, Simpson didn't want to be the reason the man lived his last moments in horrific agony.

Simpson made the call, and jabbed the syringe into the meat of Torres' remaining thigh, squeezing the tube. He tossed the tube in the dirt. Next, he pulled a sharpie from his gear pouch, writing the letters M and T on Torres' forehead, and the approximate time that he had applied both the morphine and the tourniquet. He knew the doctors could use that information to determine if they were going to have to take the rest of the limb or not. He did not know if they needed to know when morphine was administered, but figured it couldn't hurt to make it known.

Torres' cries of pain had died down considerably, and Simpson wasn't sure what to make of that. He figured it could be a good thing or a bad thing. With Torres now making less noise, he could pick out the sounds of other men screaming in pain. It was no surprise that Doc hadn't been able to get to them. Clearly he was occupied.

Muffled sounds came from inside the MRAP.

Torres was in front of him, Stevens' lifeless husk laying in the dirt just behind them. There had been only one other man in the truck.

Huggies was alive.

* * *

Once the initial blast had hit the vehicle, the three vehicles behind it had all come to rolling stops. The Marines inside the trucks got out and scanned the area around them for additional IED's. The insurgents knew the Marines' tactics almost as well as the Marines did, so a second IED was not uncommon. It was their responsibility to get to the men in the lead truck, but they had to do it safely. That would take time. When the Marines behind the ravaged vehicle began conducting their searches, the enemy insurgents struck, using the walls and huts of the nearby houses for cover and concealment. With an enemy ambush underway, the Marines in the lead vehicle would have to fend for themselves for the time being.

* * *

The concussive force of the explosion turned Ray's world black, rendering him unconscious. After a short time, his mind clawed its way out of the abyss and back to reality. Confused, he did not know where he was, but before long the reality of the situation set in. He checked himself for injuries. Blood soaked the right leg of his trousers and his hand grazed a piece of shrapnel sticking out of his thigh.

"Fuck," Ray said, grabbing the tourniquet from his body armor, he winced, fastening it two inches above the wound, stopping the flow of blood.

His head pounded. Through the cloud of sand and dust

floating in the truck's cabin, Ray looked around, his brain doing its best to scan and process the surrounding scene. The entire front end of the truck was gone, replaced with a flaming, twisted hunk of scrap metal. The driver's side door opened and Simpson grabbed Ray by his vest, yanking him from the truck. The air outside stunk of propellant, oil, fire, and blood.

"Stay down, we're taking fire. Torres got ejected from the turret. A chopper is on the way but we need to secure the area," Simpson said.

A bullet struck the vehicle just a few inches from Ray's head.

"How bad?" Ray asked.

"Real bad. Torres is fucked up. Stevens is dead. Are you hurt?" Simpson asked as another bullet struck the dirt next to his leg.

"Yeah, I've got a tourniquet on it. There's something stuck in my leg."

Simpson looked down. He said nothing. Ray could tell Simpson thought it was bad, the look on his face spoke the words that he wouldn't. Another bullet whizzed by them, slapping the truck. Simpson grabbed Ray by his body armor, grunted, and hauled him to his feet.

"Pick up your fucking weapon and return fire," he said.

Ray got his ass into gear, picking up his weapon and taking a few shots. Despite the hunk of jagged metal protruding from his leg, which tore at the flesh and muscle with each step, he bounded toward vehicle two. The truck was still unharmed and would provide better cover from which to return fire. Its passengers were also using the vehicle for cover and engaging the enemy. He took a kneeling position, wincing as the action added stress against his already wounded leg. He placed the buttstock of the rifle in the hollow of his shoulder, raised the weapon in the incoming's gunfire's direction, and scanned for a target.

The ACOG scope rested in front of his eye, the red arrow positioned center mass on an enemy combatant. Ray controlled the speed of his exhale, careful not to jostle the weapon too much. When his lungs reached their natural pause, he squeezed the trigger. Slow and steady, just like the hundreds of hours spent drilling for this exact situation. His target dropped. More bullets struck the dirt surrounding him, others pinged off the truck mere inches from his position. The enemy had no trigger discipline. They shot their weapons with reckless abandon, never stopping to place well-aimed shots, instead relying on a hail of automatic gunfire to suppress their intended targets. The insurgents were tenacious fighters, and well trained for what they were—warfighters with no formal army. But there was a big difference between them and the Marines, and the efficiency that Uncle Sam's favorite fighting force displayed dispatching their opponents proved it.

Ray sighted in on the next target. He let his lungs fill up.

He exhaled.

He pulled the trigger.

Another one down.

Something struck Ray in the chest with substantial force, knocking him on his ass. A bullet hit him in the vest, cracking it, but failing to penetrate the body armor. He scrambled to regain his position, and another round hit, this one striking him in the arm. The adrenaline coursing through his bloodstream dampened the pain, but it still hurt like a motherfucker. Blood leaked from the wound, a crimson flower spreading on the tan sleeve of his uniform.

"Incoming!" someone yelled.

Ray never heard the whistle of the mortar round. The

THE WARRIOR RETREAT

battlefield was too chaotic. Unarticulated screams of wrath joined the wails of wounded and dying men, drowning out most other noises, making it impossible to rely on one's sense of sound. Men on both sides, Marine and insurgent alike, attacked and counter-attacked, while others among them lay dying, gasping their final breaths and making peace with whatever higher power they believed in.

Everyone seemed to find God when their lives were on the line. Hell, guys suddenly found Jesus in boot camp, a place where your life was so regimented, and so many eyes were watching what you did, you were never in any real danger. So was it really a surprise when guys who'd never been to church a day in their lives were suddenly whispering a Hail Mary before patrol, or finger fucking their rosary beads in the back of the truck? Ray had been a non-believer right up until he had applied a tourniquet on his own leg, hoping to buy himself some spare time before bleeding out. He spoke to that higher power now, praying for the safety of his brothers and the death of his enemies. Enemies who prayed for the same thing, but spoke to a different God.

After burning through two magazines, Simpson fought through his own injuries, and during a lull in the firefight hurried toward Ray, kneeling by the wounded Marine's side.

"Shit, man, this really ain't your fucking day," Simpson said

Ray smirked. "That's one way to look at it."

Simpson rummaged through Ray's first aid kit until he found a package of Quikclot. He placed the package on the ground beside them and removed his knife from its sheath at his side. "Let's get this taken care of," Simpson said, cutting Ray's uniform sleeve and tearing it off. Without warning, he tore the package open and dumped the contents all over the bullet hole in Ray's arm. It stung like a bitch, and for a

31

moment he wanted to knock Simpson's teeth down his throat, but he gritted his teeth and took it.

Pain was a good thing. In boot camp, they told you pain was weakness leaving the body. If that was the case, Ray must be pretty fucking strong by now.

"Thanks," Ray said.

"You can thank me later. For now, keep fighting, and try not to get hit again. I can't reach Doc Graham on the radio. Hell, I can't reach anyone on the local comms. For all I know, Graham could be dead right now. He wouldn't be the only one. The chopper will be here soon, but for now, assume we have no medical personnel."

"Jesus. Ok. Hit and don't get hit. What is the sitrep?"

"The sitrep," Simpson laughed. "It's fucked up, that's the sitrep. We've taken some casualties, but they're taking a lot more. We have superior firepower, but they had the element of surprise. We kill the rest of these assholes and hope to God the helo gets here before Torres dies."

Bullets continued to ping off the side of the truck, the orange glare of tracer rounds occasionally flashing. Both men shouldered their weapons and fired back, dropping three more insurgents, steadily chipping away at their numbers.

Ray saw movement behind a hut about 250 meters off to their ten o'clock. He loaded the M203 grenade launcher with a click, eye fucked the range, and fired the round. It exited the tube with a *thwoomp*. The dying screams told Ray that his aim was true. He loaded another round in the launcher, searching for a new target. It didn't take long. A little further back from the first, standing on the crest of a hill, another enemy combatant. It was difficult to tell, but it looked like the man was setting something up, possibly a mortar. Ray took aim, using the leaf sight, pointing the weapon higher than before to account for the additional distance, and the higher elevation of the target. The round struck the ground about fifteen meters to the right of the man on the hill. Outside of the effective kill range, but close enough to do damage. The hillside exploded along with the round, sending the man flying. He might not be dead, but his day had just gone to hell in a handbasket.

"Nice shot," Simpson said as he fired two more rounds.

The scent of blood and cordite was overwhelming. The explosion had scrambled Ray's brains. The damage that the IED had done to his ear drums compounded along with the constant staccato of automatic gunfire, both from the enemy's AK47's and the Marines' machine guns left Ray dealing with a constant ringing in his ears that made it difficult to focus on anything, and harder still to hear the surrounding voices. Ray was experiencing tunnel vision, common to men and women in the middle of a firefight. Simpson spoke to him, but the barrage of constant auditory stimulation had taken a toll. Ray stared off in the direction where he had fired the M203 rounds, no longer searching for targets. He was zoned out, his mind blank, much like his stare.

Simpson punched Ray in the arm, the pain reverberating down the entirety of it, the impact of the blow lighting a fire in his arm where the bullet had struck him earlier.

The punch snapped Ray out of his trance.

Simpson said, "Huggies, they just keep coming. If we don't clear them out there won't be anyone left to get in the chopper."

"Yeah, you're right. Get behind the .50 cal. We need the support now!" Ray shouted.

As Simpson ran back to the smoldering ruins of their truck, Ray provided cover fire for him, allowing him the precious time he needed to get in the truck and get behind the gun. Ray watched as a seemingly endless string of insurgents came running from the huts, firing their AK47's at the Marines. Ray heard Simpson rack the M2 .50 cal machine gun. The staccato rang off as the hail of machine gun fire struck the assailants, shattering bone and literally rupturing bodies, turning them into nothing more than chunks of flesh and pink mist in the air.

It was a horrible sight to behold. Ray had only seen an M2 fired at shooting ranges before. He had heard the term "pink mist" previously, but he thought it was just some bull-shit jargon people used. Never had he considered that the massive rounds would literally turn a human body into exactly that. While horrific, Ray couldn't be happier. The insurgents had hit them hard and fast, and left them on the back foot. The Marines had fought ferociously, but there seemed to be more insurgents here than they had fought the entire deployment, and the ones that were here were clearly better trained than any of the men they had previously met on the battlefield.

"Fuck yeah, Simpson, get some!" Ray called out. Simpson didn't reply, probably couldn't hear anything over the sound of the .50. Ray smiled, knowing that Simpson's body had gone into autopilot on the machine gun. Muscle memory from drill after drill after drill ensured that what Simpson was doing took no more effort other than breathing. He was slaying bodies as mindlessly as one wiped their ass.

Ray wondered what that said about all of them that they could kill with such indifference; whether or not in a war, killing was killing.

Ray watched in awe as the machine gun continued mowing down bodies, creating a rain of viscera and bone splinters. Brain matter, internal organs, all of it turned to a pulpy mess of unidentifiable human remains.

Entranced with the real life action movie playing before

his eyes, Ray never saw the insurgent on the hill take aim at him.

The RPG made its way across the battlefield, striking the truck and sending shrapnel into the vehicle, and flying through the surrounding air. Ray heard the impact and felt himself flying before his world went black.

FOUR
THE AFTERMATH

Ray opened his eyes. A burning white light blinded him. His head pounded something fierce. A combination of injuries sustained in combat, and the sudden influx of bright light into his pupils left his brain feeling like it was caught in a vice grip. His mouth was dry and tasted like cat piss. Not that Ray had ever drank cat piss, but he'd imagined this is what his mouth would taste like if he *had* drank cat piss. He turned his head side to side, quickly scanning the room and making note of his surroundings. Nothing but medical equipment and plenty of open space. Ray could see tubes and wires running their course from different points of his body, winding around and ending at various machines which beeped and booped. What the fuck those noises meant, Ray had no clue. But seeing as he was lying in a hospital bed, he knew it couldn't be anything good.

Where am I?

Slowly, the memories came back. The dead woman. QRF being activated. Struggling to stay awake while driving. It all came flooding back. The blood, the explosions, the death.

One had to look no further than a firefight to find hell on earth.

"Ahh, you're awake," a voice said. "I'm Dr. Fonseca. I've been looking over you since you arrived in Germany. It was touch and go for quite some time, and I wasn't sure if you were going to pull through, but then something changed. Instead of a turn for the worse, you took the opposite road, and it seems now that the worst may be behind you. As it stands you aren't out of the woods, but I believe you will make a full recovery. The blast from the RPG was not as damaging as it should have been, although you sustained injuries from it. Had the round not been compromised, you and I would not be having this conversation. Lucky for you, the insurgent weaponry is not properly cared for. Had the RPG that struck the truck been in good condition, it would be a different story. You suffered multiple gunshot wounds, a concussion, and we removed multiple pieces of shrapnel from your body. Some of the shrapnel remains inside of your body, as removal could prove... complicated. At the present time, we think it best to monitor the foreign bodies, and only remove if the situation takes a turn."

Ray said nothing in response. What could he say? He was somewhere in Germany lying in a hospital bed where he had apparently been within an inch of his life until he made a miraculous recovery. Further thought brought him to the only thing he could think of to say. "Thank you, Doctor."

Dr. Fonseca cleared her throat. "Yes, well, I'm just doing my job. We've saved your legs. The tourniquet you had placed yourself held true, and likely saved you from bleeding out, but more surgeries will be required. You're also fighting an infection. I won't lie, your legs are safe for the time being, but if the infection doesn't go away, we may still take them."

Ray, again at a loss for words, said nothing. Dr. Fonseca

continued. "I told you earlier that you had suffered a concussion, but the extent of the head trauma is more severe than a simple concussion, not that a concussion is something to joke about. You suffered severe head trauma from the IED, and the many explosions that you were in close quarters to. You've been in a coma for three weeks now. How are you feeling?"

Three weeks? What happened to everyone else?

"What about the rest of my squad," Ray said.

Dr. Fonseca shook her head. "Lance Corporal Hughes, that is information that I am not privy to. Unfortunately, until someone from your chain of command arrives to meet with you, I don't have a way of getting that information to you."

Ray was pissed. He knew he should be thankful to have fared as well as he had, but he did not know how many casualties his squad had taken. He remembered Stevens died, and Torres had gotten his leg blown off. As for the rest of the squad, he had no idea the extent of the damage done to their unit.

"I'll have the nurse get you some ice chips," Dr. Fonseca said. "You're on quite a bit of medication at the moment, and have been getting your nutrients intravenously. Let's start small, and work you up to food and drink, ok?"

"Three weeks of IV fluid. I guess that explains why my mouth tastes like a litter box."

"Get some rest, Lance Corporal," Dr. Fonseca said. Ray watched as she left the room. The magic of hospital grade narcotics took hold again, making the world around him fuzzy.

Darkness took him again.

* * *

S impson grabbed the picnic bench and walked backward, dragging the bench along with him.

His blood boiled, and it was all he could do to not scream.

He had spent two weeks in Germany, recovering from wounds sustained in the ambush. Had he been so inclined, he could have used his wounds as a one-way ticket back to the United States, away from the bloodshed and tears. But he couldn't do that. His body was still in fighting shape and his platoon had taken heavy casualties. They needed all the help they could get. Aside from Stevens, two other Marines had been killed, and a handful more had been injured. Mostly, the men were patched up and back in business.

All but one had returned. Simpson worried about his friend, Hughes. He had sustained multiple wounds, more than one of them life threatening. Nobody in the battalion had bothered to inform the Marines of Hughes' condition. Simpson took that as a bad sign.

As he continued pulling the picnic bench back toward the tent, he hoped Ray would be ok. He was being overly negative. Given the situation, he thought negativity was a normal response.

Around 0600 in the morning, the company first sergeant had tasked Simpson with building the memorials for the fallen Marines. They were to look essentially like an easel, and hold a blown-up photograph of each fallen Marine. There were to be three of them, one for each man who had lost his life.

The task should have been easy, but the combat engineers claimed they had no wood on site, and would not be receiving a shipment soon. Simpson had asked them what he should tell the first sergeant, and one of those POG fucks had actually responded "Tell the first sergeant he has a better chance of finding God. Or his dick." The little fucker thought his own joke was funny, laughing hysterically. Simpson couldn't believe it. He knew that POG's like to make things difficult for grunts when they could. It was their way of saying "See, you guys need us. We're serving honorably, too." Well, the comedian found out real quick what Marcus Simpson was about, and stopped laughing when Simpson knocked his ass out cold. Then it was Simpson who was laughing. The engineers ran to their first lieutenant, who tried to stop Simpson, but he kept walking. He didn't give a shit who was talking to him. His friends were dead, and he needed to build a memorial.

On his way back to the tent, he had seen a large wooden table, and a few benches. The officers used the spot as a rec area, a place to smoke and joke away from the enlisted Marines. Simpson decided he was going to strategically relocate those items from them. As far as he was concerned, those pencil pushing pussies never saw combat a day in their lives, so they didn't need an opportunity to relax. They could eat shit. And if they tried to stop him, Simpson would make them do just that.

Simpson made it back to the Weapons Company area with the picnic bench in tow. He brought it around to the back end of their tent, free from spying eyes and anyone who might snitch. There were plenty of ass-kissers around, and if word got out that their shit was missing, there would inevitably be some brown-nosing Marine looking to get a meritorious promotion.

Behind the tent, there was a small toolbox. Simpson grabbed a hammer, some nails, a tape measure, and a small handsaw from the chest. With the materials and the tools now acquired, Simpson began the arduous task of breaking down

41

all the furniture, nail by nail, and reshaping it into something worthy to see his friends off to Valhalla.

The sun had set hours ago, but it was hot as hell, and within a few minutes sweat saturated Simpson's clothing. His skivvy shirt stuck to his back and felt trickles of the warm bodily secretion dripping down the crack of his ass. The heat ravaged him, but he didn't care. He chugged water from his canteen and continued breaking the bench down piece by piece until it was nothing more than long planks of wood.

With the furniture broken down to its base form, he sketched up some haphazardly drawn plans for making the easels. Simpson wasn't a carpenter, and he sure as shit wasn't an artist, but he wasn't about to let anything stop him from putting the memorial together. Even if the final product turned out like absolute shit—and there was no doubt in his mind it would turn out exactly as such—he was going to complete the task at hand for his brothers. They fought along-side him and made the ultimate sacrifice. For that, Simpson felt that going outside of his wheelhouse to make the best damn shitty memorial he could make was the least he could do.

* * *

The sun dipped below the horizon just as the memorial service concluded. Simpson had volunteered to take part in the ceremony and had spent the better part of a week practicing drill whenever there was downtime between patrols. Building the memorial stands wasn't enough; he needed to take part in it, too. He skipped meals and briefings. Hell, he skipped basic personal hygiene. It had been days since he had showered, despite the new showers the engineers had built. Every waking hour was spent on patrol, and perfecting drill maneuvers.

Simpson's hard work had paid off, his drill so crisp you'd be forgiven for thinking he just graduated boot camp.

Not that drill counted for anything. He couldn't help but wonder if he had wasted his time. Yes, the ceremony went off without a hitch, and despite the shoddy looking picture memorials, the ceremony itself was impressive. Immaculate. But that wouldn't bring his brothers back. And Simpson wasn't sure what the point of this was anymore.

For his heroic actions on the battlefield, the Marine Corps intended on awarding him a bronze star, with a V for valor. Other men who had been on patrol that day would be awarded as well, and as far as Simpson knew Lance Corporal Robert Haney was also set to receive a bronze star. Haney had been in the rear truck with Micha, and from the details of the after action report had put plenty of bodies in the dirt himself. They were war heroes, and would be awarded as such. Simpson didn't want an award for killing anyone; he wanted his friends back. The battalion commander told him to think about the lives he had saved, but how could he do that when every night he closed his eyes only to see the faces of the men he *couldn't* save.

Simpson inhaled, taking in the toxic fumes of the burning trash just outside of the HESCO barriers. Nothing like pre-ordering a ticket for cancer later on down the road. Everyone knew burn pits were toxic, but the government wasn't really doing anything to keep service members safe from them. When it came down to it, things needed to be disposed of, and burning those things was the only way to get rid of them. The military didn't give a shit about them, or the planet. By the time the United States Government is ready to take action on burn pit hazards, there will already have been plenty of cases of rare cancers and fucked up diseases littering the medical charts of men and women who served on bases such as the one Simpson found himself.

Between dying a brutal death, suicides, or fucked up medical issues, he thought the war would punch the ticket of everyone who served, eventually.

Wanting to calm his nerves, Simpson pulled a can of dip from his pocket. He flicked his wrist, packing the can of Grizzly wintergreen. Grizz-Daddy was his poison of choice, guaranteed to put hair on your nuts. Using his index and middle fingers, Simpson scooped a generous amount and packed his lower lip as tight as he could. His lip protruded comically, and although he wouldn't be caught dead dipping if he was back home in Rhode Island, he held a secret love for the nasty habit, something he had picked up all the way back during the School of Infantry training.

That felt like an entire lifetime ago. And in some ways, it was.

"Hey there, Devil Dog," called a voice from behind.

Great, what now?

When you got hit with the "Devil Dog" moniker, you knew you were in for an ass chewing. Some dickhead, too proud of his rank—often a staff NCO or an officer—wanted to dig in your ass for some reason.

Today was not the day to try Marcus Simpson.

He ignored the call, kept his head down and his feet moving. He hoped that ignoring the man would make him go away, but he knew he had a better chance of seeing Jesus Christ himself in the porta shitters. The higher ups lived for moments like this. "Correcting" a junior Marine was practically a fucking orgasmic experience to them. Hell, Simpson wouldn't be surprised to look down and see one of these sick fucks popping a chub mid ass chewing.

A hand clamped down on Simpson's shoulder. "Hey there, Mar..."

Simpson spun around, swinging for the fences as he did so. His fist collided with the Marine's—who turned out to be Lieutenant Cobb—jaw, smashing it closed with an audible click. The punch knocked a tooth free, and the Lieutenant swallowed it as his head whipped violently to the side.

Lieutenant Cobb quickly recovered and struck back, using his calves to stand on his toes, propelling his skull upward into Simpson's nose, which had only recently felt better after breaking it against the truck during the ambush a few weeks ago. A gout of blood sprayed forth as the nose shattered again, covering both Marines.

Simpson cried out, the pain of re-breaking the nose excruciating. He speared Cobb, taking him to the ground and mounting him, using his full body weight to pin the Lieutenant's arms beneath his knees. Having the upper hand, he teed off. Unable to buck Simpson off, Cobb was defenseless, forced to eat shot after shot from the large, angry Marine.

Simpson's vision red with rage, he was at the mercy of his own emotions, powerless to stop himself from pummeling the lieutenant. And he himself was also powerless to stop what was happening.

"Hey! Knock it off!" Sergeant Finger called as he sprinted toward the Marines, hopping on Simpson's back. It took all of Finger's strength to pull Simpson off Cobb, and even then, Simpson would not stop. He twisted and turned, trying to buck Finger off of him, while still trying to get a few more shots at Cobb. Mark and Paul, coming back from chow, saw the ruckus and helped to subdue Simpson.

A Navy Corpsman responded to Finger's yells for medical, kneeling over Cobb, assessing the ass whooping that Simpson had doled out.

As the tide of anger that had washed over Simpson slowly receded, the realization of what he had done gradually hit him.

He had taken his anger out on another Marine, common enough on a combat deployment. But it wasn't the fact that he had fought another Marine—that shit could be swept under the rug—but he'd assaulted a commissioned officer. *That shit* was *never* swept under the rug. It was used as an example.

Simpson would be lucky to *not* fry for his actions. The hellacious ass whooping he had dished out to Cobb was something the lieutenant had no real chance of preventing. Simpson was a beast. But you bet your ass Lieutenant Cobb was going to shove Simpson's shit in with a mound of paperwork as large as Simpson himself.

Sergeant Finger escorted Simpson to the company first sergeant's tent. Simpson was surprised that Finger hadn't bothered to talk him down, to tell him everything would be ok.

In hindsight, Simpson knew Finger was just keeping it real. There would be no smoothing this one over, so why bother lying?

Simpson didn't know it at the time, but the assault marked the beginning of the end of his career in the Marine Corps.

Sergeant Finger, knowing first-hand about combat experience and the emotions that drove Simpson's actions—something the lieutenant would never know about—worked tirelessly to keep Simpson out of the brig, and to convince the company first sergeant to skip a court martial expulsion, and instead pursue a medical discharge. In the end Finger worked a bit of magic, and although he could not prevent a separation of service, he *was* successful in his attempts to change the method of discharge, allowing Simpson, who had proven himself a war hero, to exit the Marine Corps and keep his benefits.

The only men who would ever know the truth of the stain on Simpson's career would let it die overseas, along with the dozens of men Weapons Company would lose during their seven-month tour.

PART TWO
THE WAR AT HOME

FIVE
THE ADVOCATE

F*ive years later*
The air conditioning unit struggled to keep up with the heat and humidity of Simpson's apartment, despite it being cranked to the max. It was downright oppressive and disgusting. The third-floor apartment could get hotter than Satan's taint. Hell, Simpson had the AC cranking in the winter just to offset how warm it got from the apartments below him running their heat all day long. At the time he had secured the lease, Simpson was simply happy to have a place of his own, without government assistance.

He chalked it up as a lesson learned.

Since being forced out of the Marine Corps, Simpson had quite a few "learning" moments. Dealing with PTSD was an everyday struggle, but those early days were absolute hell, dating back to the day that he beat the ever-loving shit out of Lieutenant Cobb. Yes, he was a hothead. He was a product of an upbringing where it was learn to fight or get used to getting your ass whooped. Simpson decided as a young kid he didn't much care for being on the receiving end of ass whoopings. The events that transpired overseas, culminating with his separation, were nothing more than the result of taking a scrappy city kid, training him to become a hard ass killer, and then subjecting him to an onslaught of traumatic experiences.

His struggles had only worsened when he was shipped back home to Rhode Island. It was touch and go for about a year, in and out of jail numerous times, his record as a war hero the only thing keeping him from doing serious time. But his luck had run out, and the last time Simpson appeared before a judge, they strongly impressed it upon him that his chances had run dry. He could either shape up, or the next time he appeared before the court he should be prepared to do a significant amount of time.

Message received.

Simpson spent the next four years working with psychologists and psychiatrists at the Providence VA Medical Center. As the treatment dragged Simpson out of his downward spiral and put him on an upward trajectory, he used his post 9/11 GI bill benefits and pursued a degree in social work. It was a long, arduous road, and sometimes he wanted to give up, but he dug his feet in and pushed through. Now, he was proud to say that he was a social worker specializing in veterans advocacy. Much of what he did involved getting vets the help they needed, whatever, or wherever that may be. It wasn't just limited to the VA; if guys needed substance abuse programs, he could get them in. If guys needed housing help, he could connect them with the resources necessary. Hell, he could get you into marriage counseling if that's what you needed, even though he hadn't been able to save his own marriage.

His son, Anthony, was the only good thing that had come from that marriage, and the sole reason that he wound up straightening his life out. He didn't give a rat's ass about his wife, or winning her back. Anthony and his advocacy work were the only priorities in his life.

Simpson closed his laptop, stretching his arms and moaning. He had just completed a project that had been in the pipeline for quite some time. Using his advocacy connections, Simpson got a nonprofit organization called Leathernecks for Leathernecks to fund a retreat for himself and a few of the Marines he had served with. Readjusting to civilian life was difficult, and there were many who failed. He knew from experience. Some of his brothers still struggle, and he was determined to help them.

Initially, Simpson had been unsure how many of his brothers could attend; it's difficult to get guys—some of whom didn't have a pot to piss in—to commit to traveling across the United States for a reunion. But LFL offered to fund transportation to get everyone safely on site. Nobody had an excuse to not show up at this point.

There was one man, above all others, that Simpson hoped would make the trip—Ray. Except could you call it a trip when the retreat was being held within an hour drive from where the guy lived? Simpson didn't think so, and that was precisely why he found a cabin in the middle of nowhere, on a lake in Rhode Island.

Secluded in Rhode Island didn't really mean the same thing it did in other states. Sure they would be in the middle of the woods, but it was easily accessible from anywhere in the state.

Simpson felt bad that he didn't see Ray much anymore. They both lived in Rhode Island, and could easily carve out plans, but life doesn't always work that way. Things change, and eventually it becomes easy to find excuses on why you *can't* do something rather than make the time to do it. Simpson knew that any excuses he made on why they didn't get together were pure bullshit. Ray was struggling, he knew it, and if Ray wanted to make it difficult to make plans, Simpson could have just shown up.

But he didn't. That was something Simpson had been working on in his own therapy sessions. He still felt like he had failed Ray all those years ago, and a part of him believed that if he were to confront Ray now, and see with his own two eyes that Ray was doing as bad as he had heard, that it would bring back all of his own baggage, and torpedo the strides he had made with his own mental wellbeing.

Simply put, Marcus Simpson was afraid that he would lose himself again.

But Ray didn't make helping him easy, either. He went through phone numbers like a whore went through condoms, and if you managed to get the correct number, he never answered it. If you shot the guy a text message, he might text you back a week later. Or not at all.

Simpson let those thoughts run through his mind for a minute, and then punted them from his brain. All he was doing by thinking like that was making excuses and putting the blame on Ray. Simpson knew damn well that most veterans who needed help withdrew, rarely seeking the help they needed.

The thing that concerned Simpson the most about Ray's wellbeing was the man's inclination to say some truly unnerving things. The few times they'd actually had a conversation, Ray had mentioned crazy shit, something about a ghost that haunted him. He told Simpson of an elaborate story about waking up one night in Iraq to the haunting. And he blamed the lack of sleep which ultimately led to him running over the IED, on this "haunting."

Simpson knew Ray was experiencing delusions, night terrors, all linked back to traumatic events overseas. But to

Ray, they were real. He knew that Ray's problem lie in something called "Sleep Paralysis," but the problem was convincing a man who had been traumatized that it was nothing more than a nightmare.

The wounds Ray sustained that day five years ago were only the start. While there was no way to prove it, Simpson believed Ray to be a prime Chronic Traumatic Encephalopathy candidate, and delusions were simply proof of that. The man had been blown up a half dozen times *before* that day, for Christ's sake. A person doesn't walk away from that type of concussive trauma without leaving bits and pieces of their sanity in the desert.

Still, in order to help Ray it would require him to actually attend the retreat, something that held similar odds as winning the Powerball. If Simpson even managed to get ahold of Ray, the man would likely commit to the retreat, then pull a disappearing act at the last minute.

It was a shame, brave men and women put their lives on the line in service of their country, but all too often the ones who come home have left so much behind that sometimes Simpson wondered if they wouldn't have been better off dy... no, he couldn't let those thoughts take root. If he did, he might as well quit his job now. His work was for nothing if he truly believed that.

He wouldn't fail Ray again.

SIX
FIRST ROUND KNOCKOUT

The bar was packed. Ray did his best to distance himself from the crowd, but when a place had as many patrons as the bar had tonight, solitude was not an option. He settled for a chair in the rear corner of the bar. Stuck in the corner, surrounded by a sea of drunks, the claustrophobia hit him hard. He scrunched his shoulders, trying to shrink himself so he would feel less crowded, but when you were as large a man as Ray, there was no creating a smaller profile.

The hot, stale air did nothing to ease the feeling, and Ray kicked himself in the ass for choosing the corner seat on this night. The only reason he had selected the corner was the fact that it allowed him to see all points of entry and exit to the building, providing a full view of the room and anyone who might sneak up on him. He didn't do well in crowds, and he didn't do well with people standing behind him.

The bartender, Melonie, approached Ray. "What can I get ya?"

"A shot of Tito's, a Jack and Coke, and a Bud Light, please."

Mel nodded her head, while giving him a disapproving look. "Cash or tab?"

"Tab."

Ray knew that look. She was trying to decide if he was going to be a problem, or if he could hold his liquor. They weren't supposed to serve more than two drinks to a single person, but most of the time, so long as you weren't already shitfaced or a known douchebag, the local bars would turn a blind eye to that rule. Bartending was a service that ran on tips and there was no better way to sabotage your tip than to turn down a customer.

Ray watched Mel pour his drinks, letting his gaze linger on her ample ass. He broke his gaze as she made her way back with his drinks.

She placed them on the countertop. "Hope you didn't break your jaw when it hit the floor." Mel placed the drinks in front of Ray, who placed his card on the countertop. "You want to keep it open, baby?" she asked.

"Yep," he said. Ray knew she meant nothing by calling him "baby," it was another tactic to maximize her tips. Chat the women up, flirt with the men. The problem was that most men were too stupid to realize it was all part of the game. Ray knew the game, but he still took the charm hook, line, and sinker.

Ray had no interest in pursuing anything further, with Melonie or any woman. Half the time he could barely get himself out of bed in the morning. He was a shitshow, and didn't take care of himself. Tonight, he was halfway presentable, but he was well aware of the way he presented himself, even on nights he cleaned up.

Besides, even if Ray decided to shoot his shot, he had the incredible luck of being one of the tiny percentage of men somehow still experiencing ED for months after coming off of antidepressants. The pills were supposed to help him, but no matter what they switched him to, the side effects seemed worse than the ailment. He would rather be depressed, anxious, and hot-headed than walk around feeling like a zombie stuck in a cloud, so he stopped using antidepressants only to discover they had gotten him a gift that keeps on giving.

The last time he spoke with a doctor about the predicament with his pickle, the urologist broke the horrific news that in rare cases, some men experience ED for *years* after coming off of an SSRI. Ray didn't think he'd last *years* without at least rubbing one out. Just thinking about it made him want to die, and that was on top of his already crippling mental health issues. And while Ray didn't expect a relationship with anyone given his lack of self-care and his ongoing mental issues, it would be nice to crank one out, or pick up a hooker every once in a while.

He slurped the mixed drink down in two long gulps and took a swig from the beer. The alcohol had already helped to take the edge off of his anxiety, so Ray signaled Mel for another round while polishing off the Bud.

The man sitting on the stool next to Ray watched in wide-eyed amazement, making no attempt to hide the fact that he was staring. "Hey, buddy, it's only eight o'clock. Keep that up, you're going to be all the way in the bag before the preliminary fights start."

Ray ignored the man, and although he had to admit that the nosy piece of shit beside him had a point, he would not let that deter him from getting obliterated. Getting absolutely annihilated and watching the fights had become something of a ritual to Ray and his squad mates all those years ago. Back in Hawaii, those had usually been MMA fights. Here in Rhode Island, he had taken to boxing and followed the sport religiously, although it was a complete dumpster fire of bull-shit and sports politics. It had to be the most corrupt sport on the planet, and the same sharks that bled the athletes for all they were worth actively turned a wider audience *away* from it with the toxic and, frankly, confusing way they ran the sport.

Those old bastards leeching off the fighters could get their faces fucked, as far as Ray was concerned. He'd have stopped watching if it weren't for the blood and guts way in which some men fought in the ring. Tonight was one of those nights where you knew you were about to see a war. Orlando Salido and Francisco Vargas were fighting, and there was no way in hell the fight would not be a barnburner.

The man beside Ray seemed unable to take a hint, and would not be denied his conversation. "Not much of a talker are ya, bud?" the man said.

Ray sucked his teeth, irritated at the asshole's insistence on chatting him up. If this douche nozzle was going to inject himself into Ray's personal space throughout the night, there would be a blood and guts affair in the parking lot, that was for sure.

As Ray sucked down the drinks, the alcohol took hold of his body, and much as he hated to admit it, he was getting tired before the main event even started. That fucker next to him had jinxed him. Ray waved Melonie over. He needed a change of pace. A pick me up. He ordered a Red Bull and vodka. A few of these would bring him zero to sixty and keep him up well into the early hours of the morning. He loved the way the energy drink kept him afloat long past the point when the alcohol should have put him out of commission, and not only that, but the drink tasted like candy. The only downside to the heavenly mixture—it seemed as if every awful experi-ence he'd ever had with alcohol had involved that drink.

Fuck it. What's the worst that can happen?

* * *

The fight was over. When it was all said and done, both men's hands' raised in a draw. Somehow, inexplicably, after beating the ever-loving shit out of each other for twelve rounds, both men ended the fight on their own two feet. What a night.

Somehow, inexplicably, after Ray went twelve rounds of drinks, he too ended the night on his own two feet.

He stood outside of Billy's Frosted Mug, better known to locals as "The Frosted Thug". There was no real reason for the nickname. One of the bar's regulars had said it joking around one day and somehow the name had stuck. Even the owner called it by the nickname now.

Ray smoked a cigarette with Bobby, the area's resident coke dealer. The Frosted Thug was the type of establishment where the upper and lower-class citizens mingled, sharing alcohol and drugs like they were best friends.

Ray had consumed enough alcohol to kill a lesser man, but it allowed him to be around the crowd of people without having an anxiety attack. It had only taken over a hundred dollars-worth of liquor to dampen the PTSD enough to allow him to function in public.

The fight had everyone amped up, even the people who didn't give a shit about combat sports. It seemed like half the bar stuck around to shoot the shit and smoke a stogie, talking about the brutal display that had been on the bar's televisions. There was nothing quite like two guys beating the shit out of each other for your viewing pleasure, and the electric atmosphere outside of The Frosted Thug proved it. They shared their laughter, their cigarettes, their weed, and—if the woman on her knees sucking cock was any sign—their bodily fluids as well.

Ray put the cigarette out on the wall and threw the butt on the ground. He was about ready to head home for the night and pass out when Bobby sparked a blunt, took a hit and passed it to him. Never one to pass up free drugs, Ray accepted the joint and put it to his lips, taking a long pull from the blunt while he watched the woman on her knees work the balls and deepthroat the shaft. Ray didn't want to be a pervert, but he was so shocked at what transpired that he couldn't look away. This was the first time he'd seen a complete stranger gobbling a cock in public before. He supposed it probably happened more than he realized, but the sight of it was unexpected.

Ray held the blunt out, returning it to Bobby, when someone bumped into him from behind, knocking the blunt from his hand and into a puddle on the ground.

"What the fuck," Ray said, turning around and coming face to face with the klutz who had bumped into him. It was the dickhead from the bar that wouldn't leave him be.

"Wow, you can talk?" the guy said. He smiled at Ray. "I thought you were a fucking mute or something."

Ray inhaled deeply, resisting the urge to choke the shit out of the asshole.

The klutz laughed again and nodded his head in the direction of the woman swallowing a load. "You keep watching her over there. Are you trying to learn some tips?" He continued laughing, ignorant to the fact that the newly gathered audience was not laughing at his homophobic joke.

Ray didn't give him a chance to say another word. He closed the homophobes mouth with his bear-paw like fist, shattering the front teeth and sending blood spewing forth from his mouth like a faucet left to run. The asshole fell flat on his ass, pants soaked from the water on the ground.

Ray had enough trouble controlling his anger when he hadn't consumed enough alcohol to keep a small army intoxicated. Throwing alcohol in the mix was bad news, and the homophobe choking on his teeth was a testament to Ray's constantly lit short fuse.

He showed his heckler no quarter, snatching him up from the ground by the collar and using his free fist to pummel the smartass. Two more punches connected with a sickening thud, and although Ray didn't need to use full force on the man, he was seeing red and couldn't have lightened up if he wanted to.

Cocking back his fist once more, Ray launched a punch so hard it was like he was trying to punch *through* the man, sending him reeling backward, smacking his head against the building, where he crumpled to the ground like a wet paper bag. A newly rearranged nose complimented the man's broken teeth and shattered orbital bone. His face was unrecognizable.

The sound of distant police sirens sent the crowd scattering to the four corners of the earth, snapping Ray out of his frenzy.

He looked at the bleeding and battered man, wondering if he was dead. He certainly looked that way, and it took a few moments of hard staring to spot the shallow rise and fall of his chest. The man was alive, but would he stay that way?

"Get out of here, man," Bobby said. "This place doesn't have any cameras."

Ray didn't even consider the consequences, hauling ass out of the parking lot, zipping through the side streets and doing his best to avoid the police.

SEVEN
22 A DAY

The moonlight infiltrated the cracks and crevices of the dingy blinds in Eric Torres' shitty, run down dump of a studio apartment. The lunar luminesce provided the only source of illumination. He liked it that way. In the sunlight, everything was front and center. His haggard, gaunt cheeks. The filth and grime one acquired when they went days without washing themselves.

It exposed the atrocious conditions he lived in. Refuse littered the room. Days' old leftovers rotting in the heat of the sweltering apartment. Rat and mice droppings scattered throughout the kitchen, where they regularly chewed through the packages of food in the cabinets. Roaches scurrying across every surface. No, he didn't need the lights on. He knew he was a slob. A scumbag. Torres saw no need to shine a light on that fact.

He took a long pull from the bottle of Knob Creek as he read through his email for the third time today. He gagged. Maybe from the bite of the bourbon, or maybe the horrid stench emanating from every surface had engaged his gag reflex. Hell, it was entirely possible an extra strong whiff of the onion-like stench of his unwashed body had turned his stomach, threatening to purge its contents at any moment.

Over the past few days, he had read the email Simpson had sent him at least a couple dozen times. He had even replied to it and told Simpson of course he would love to go to the retreat. Torres had typed the obligatory enthusiastic response, feigning excitement.

Of course he would love to meet up with the guys, bullshit with everyone.

It would be great to hobble on over and pretend like nothing had ever happened. Like the trip would be just another weekend with the boys. Nothing he'd rather do than smoke and joke with his old buddies from the 'Corps!

But in reality, when he thought long and hard about the prospects of coming face to face with his old buddies, and being forced to relive everything he chose to forget through self-medication, it was the last thing on this fucking planet he wanted to do. Every day for the last five years, all he had to do was look down to his stump, that hideous lump of flesh where his leg had once been, and it reminded him all about the good old days. Reminded him of a time when he had signed up to defend his country, because it was the patriotic thing to do. Because his country needed him to fight the terrorists.

But what they didn't tell you was that much of the fighting would not be done against terrorists, or anyone who had anything to do with September 11th. Nope, you would fight "insurgents" some of whom had ties to the fabled terrorists the news spoke of, but many of whom were people who were forced by the *actual* terrorists to attack coalition forces, or they were citizens who had simply had enough of occupying forces in their homeland.

But it wasn't patriotism that had caused him to enlist in

the Marine Corps. He didn't give a rat's ass about America, a country that didn't give a flying fuck about him. He knew what so many people thought about Mexican Americans. Racism was not gone, it was not over. Maybe things were better today than they were for his parents and grandparents, but that didn't mean things were *good*.

No, Eric Torres had enlisted in the Marine Corps because he was smart enough to know that the post 9-11 GI bill was a phenomenal opportunity. Four years of his life for four years of college. It was the only way he was going to get a higher education without undertaking a crippling debt. He was smart enough to know that it made little sense to rack-up tens, maybe hundreds of thousands in student loan debt to get a job that paid fifty grand a year. Let the government pay for it. Imagine the irony of worrying about crippling debit...only to come back crippled!

And the plan would have worked, but Torres had fucked up. He'd gotten high with a friend before boot camp, and he thought that there would be enough time for it to clear his system. Boy was he wrong. He took a piss test upon arrival, and a few days later had been informed that he had failed. Happens all the time, but there was one minor problem. During the moment of truth, where they specifically ask you if you had a little fun before you stepped on those yellow footprints, Torres, thinking the weed was already out of his system, had lied.

He wasn't just a pot smoker, now he was an *integrity violator*. But don't worry, there's good news! We aren't kicking you out of the Corps, son! They're just going to tear up that contract, the one that you signed to become an intelligence Marine, and they're going to draft a new contract. You'll be an Infantryman now, one of the proudest occupations in the entire United States Military.

And the best news? Even though you smoked that pot, even though you got caught, once your four years were up, it would be like it never happened. If you kept your nose clean, you would get an honorable discharge like everyone else, and that free ride to college would still be yours.

So Torres did his time, but he didn't make it the whole contract. He'd only been in for a little over a year before his leg was turned into minced meat.

Many guys leave service and are forever proud of what they had done, of who they had become. Not Torres; Torres was a shell of a man. He had come home less than whole, both physically and mentally. He wished he was one of those men who seemed to strap on a prosthetic leg and call it a day, but he couldn't force his mind to pretend. His father used to tell him, wish in one hand, shit in the other and see what fills up first. No longer did he wonder what the fuck that meant.

Disability checks covered the rent and nothing more. After his medical discharge, Torres fought tooth and nail for disability benefits. And while yes, he received a service connected designation for his leg, PTSD, tinnitus, and hearing loss, the VA fucked him on the percentages of each condition. There was a range associated with each disability, and for each one the claims personnel he had seen had given him the lowest possible designation. And with VA math, which is nothing like *real* math. A sixty percent disability rating for one injury and a ten percent disability rating for another, separate injury, still only added up to sixty. It made no sense to anyone with a functioning brain, but it was the primary method the VA used to make sure that payouts were kept to a minimum.

With the VA disability system, not only did you see a revolving door of medical personnel, but the person actually handling your claims wasn't even the doctor who evaluated you, but some random hero who reviewed your files and got to play God, telling *you* how much your severed leg, lit fuse temper, and crippling anxiety interfered with your ability to live a normal life.

Torres had tried to get a 100-percent unable to work, but the best rating he could achieve was sixty percent on the leg, the many other injuries only adding another ten percent combined, which was bullshit because he knew men with lesser injuries, hell even fake injuries, who were all getting paid more than he was.

Was it fair? No. Was there anything he could do about it? Nothing he could think of. He'd already had VFW and DAV members work his claim. Everyone promised they could up his percentage, but in the end nobody had helped.

And wasn't that the story of the last five years? Nobody there to help. His wife had left him. When he was recovering from the IED in Germany, she had sent him a *Dear John* letter. She wanted him to know that she just couldn't take it anymore; she needed someone who was home. Someone who was whole. She had missed him so much, and now couldn't bear the thought of seeing him and his grotesque stub. And she was so sorry that he had experienced that, but it was just the way she felt, and wouldn't it be selfish of him to want her to stay when she couldn't even look at his leg anymore. And how was she supposed to have sex with a man whose missing leg made her want to puke? From there, the letter got worse.

In Torres' absence, his brother, Lester, had been kind enough to provide the emotional support for her. And equally important, as her letter made *explicitly* clear, Lester was also kind enough to provide her with—in her exact words—a freakishly huge fuck stick. She had actually written that in the letter, fuck stick.

How thoughtful of his brother, he with three legs, to

satiate his wife's uncontrollable thirst for getting her pussy destroyed.

He had tried to kill himself for the first time that day, with a vision of his brother's massive dong pounding his wife's cunt. The image replayed on a loop in his head, like a DVD that kept skipping.

And that was just the start of his long, sustained downward spiral. Every day for the last five years had been a struggle to wake up and get out of bed.

Torres didn't want to struggle anymore.

He picked up the bottle of Knob Creek one last time, chugging it in huge gulps like a frat boy shot-gunning a beer. At least the way he chugged the bottle would have made the guys proud.

Tears streamed down Torres' cheeks, leaving streaks through the grime on his unwashed face. He slammed the bottle down, hard, and it broke, shattering in his hand and slicing his palm open. He hardly felt it, and if it weren't for the warmth in his palm, he probably wouldn't have known he was bleeding.

Torres leaned over and snatched his AR-15 from the coffee table.

The weapon had not been taken care of. Fuck what you heard about never being able to remove the Corps from a Marine. Torres had cleaned enough rifles to last a lifetime. Besides, he had only purchased the weapon for one reason. Despite his best efforts to put one foot forward and start each day anew, in the back of his mind he had always known his fate.

He swiped the magazine off of the coffee table; it was loaded, although with only one round. No need for a full combat load today.

He slapped the bulky object into the magazine well,

pulled the charging handle to the rear and let go, allowing the bolt to slam forward, loading a round into the chamber.

Torres again pulled the charging handle to the rear, this time ever so slightly, making sure the round was properly seated in the chamber. He wanted to avoid a misfire today.

He placed the buttstock of the AR-15 on the floor between his knees and switched the safety selector to fire. The weapon was hot and ready to go.

So was Torres.

He wrapped his lips around the barrel and pulled the trigger one last time.

EIGHT
THE INFLUENCER

Despite all the shit that Robert Haney had been through during two combat tours—and maybe *because* of those things—he thrived. Most men struggled with their demons upon re-entry into the civilian sector, and for a brief period, Haney had been no different.

Somewhere along the line he'd gotten his shit together. Haney had put a focus and determination on his own mental wellbeing. He found solace in video games, a hobby that he had little time for when he was in the Marine Corps. Instead of sitting on his ass in a perpetual state of depression and anxiety, he doubled down on self-motivation and pulled himself up from the depths of despair, using his post 9/11 GI Bill benefits to go back to school.

After several years of hard work and studying his ass off, Haney obtained a bachelor's degree in communications, specializing in video editing. Hard work and dedication was something Haney had in spades, and lately he'd been able to combine those qualities with his degree, love of gaming, and a dash of good luck to create a successful online YouTube channel and streaming platform. He started the various channels a few years back, with only a bit of success, but once he had completed his degree he suddenly had the free time necessary to turn his hobby into a career. Now, Haney was on the road to becoming a millionaire.

That he was one of the few men from his squad who'd found any amount of success wasn't lost on Haney, and it was for that reason he replied "yes" to Simpson's invite without hesitation, knowing that it was going to require modification to his streaming and upload schedule—something that he typically avoided like the plague.

Part of the problem with being an "influencer" was the fact that viewers expected him to have a schedule and stick to it. Sure, plenty of streamers missed their scheduled streams, they missed upload days on their YouTube channel, but those people weren't Robert Haney, and that was why his channel was blowing up as fast as it was. He was a good-looking, charismatic man with an incredible drive for success.

Missing a day was unthinkable.

A lightbulb winked inside of Haney's mind.

What if he didn't have to drastically alter his schedule? What if he could upload a few videos, and do a live stream from the retreat? Simpson had mentioned in the initial email that he wanted this to be a gadget free weekend, but cell phones were practically appendages these days. And besides, Haney didn't think Simpson would say no. It might take some begging, but when it came down to it, whether Simpson and the guys thought it was stupid or not was irrelevant. Haney was an online personality, and keeping a tight schedule was part of his livelihood. Subscriptions, sponsors, and donations were all a part of his life, and he would have to tell Simpson creating content during the retreat was part of the deal if they expected him to make the trip.

Simpson would agree, on that, Haney was positive.

Running on fumes from an exhausting 24-hour live stream, but not wanting to go to sleep yet—he had already planned his schedule around going to bed at a certain time so he could wake up and be ready for his next scheduled stream —Haney cracked open a can of Monster Energy and navigated his web browser to his email account. The idea already planned in his mind, he put to digital paper his pitch to Simpson, all the while planning how he was going to parlay the change in setting into something his viewers could get excited about.

Haney was a tough worker, and his fans were rabid for content. He was confident he could both reunite with his brother, and produce killer content for the insatiable appetite of his viewers.

NINE
THAT HAWAII BY NIGHT MAGIC

Pumping through the low budget sound system was "In Love with a Stripper" by T-Pain. A haze of smoke filled the room. Beams of purple lighting shone through the film of cheap fog and cigarette smoke, creating an ambience that could only be found in the grimiest of grimy strip joints. The stench of piss, vomit, alcohol, and dollar store perfume lingered throughout the air, a vile concoction that you could smell the moment you walked through the door, and let you know just what type of establishment you had walked into. One where the women on stage were cheap, and the beers even cheaper.

Is that how the saying goes? Micha Menard thought as he took a swig from his Bud Light, keeping his gaze locked firmly on the center stage.

Gyrating on that stage, a twenty-something woman. Her olive complexion shone under the lighting, which reflected its illumination off of the sheen of sweat coating her body. Micha didn't know how it was possible for a woman to have the body proportions she did, but he silently thanked God for creating her as he rubbed the head of his cock with one hand and tossed a dollar bill on stage with the other.

"Really, Micha?" Mark punched Micha's arm, causing him to stop what he was doing. Micha, caught in the act, looked to the left and right, eyes wide as if he was bewildered. Like someone had caught him raiding a panty drawer. And technically, he *had* been caught doing that. But that was years ago, and they had served him a dishonorable discharge for that stunt. He had been drunk, and claimed to have no recollection of the event, and while that was true, it was no less disgusting, and by no means excused him from the behavior. And while they might have kicked him out of the Corps, they couldn't kick him out of Hawaii. Micha loved the island and refused to leave. This was his home now.

This strip club, *Hawaii By Nights*, was his second home.

"I've never seen an ass like that either, but God damn, man, can you not play with yourself at the fucking table?"

Micha didn't know what to say to that, so rather than make himself seem like even more of a shithead, he simply didn't respond to the comment.

A scantily-clad brunette approached them. Her top hardly contained her massive breasts, and her ass threatened to burst out of the scant cloth that did little to cover her.

"You fellas want to buy some shots?" she asked as she stood between the two men, intentionally placing her generous backside in front of Micha while giving Mark a prime view of the frontal wedgie she was rocking.

This woman was a pro at selling drinks. How could either of them say no when their faces were close enough to her snatch they could smell it. They purchased two shots of an unknown green liquid pre-filled in thin, clear tubes. Almost like something you'd see in a high school science lab.

Katie, or so she called herself, handed the tubes to the

guys and gave them instructions to not drink them until she was ready. Placing her tray on their table, she picked up a tube and threw back one herself.

Micha and Mark locked eyes and smiled. Katie pulled her top lower, exposing more of her cleavage. She grabbed Mark's tube and put it between her breasts. With the tube in between her tits, she squatted low, grabbed the waistband of her shorts and hiked them further up her ass, as if such a thing was even possible. She took the shot from Micha and placed it in her ample ass cheeks, leaving the top half of it poking out at an upward angle.

"Are you boys ready for some spit-roast shots?" she asked.

Both men nodded enthusiastically.

"Ok, get on your knees then," she said.

Micha knelt down, lining his mouth up with Katie's peach-shaped ass. Mark knelt down in front of her, unsure how he'd get his shot.

"Let's do this," she said, leaning forward at the waist. She pushed her ass back and up so that Micha's tube went into his mouth. He caught it in his lips, tilting his head back as her ass raised in the air, plucking the shot from those beautiful cheeks. The liquor tasted like candy as it slid down his throat. The tube itself tasted salty from Katie's sweat.

As her ass raised up, her front came down, and while Micha was drinking a shot out of her ass cheeks, Katie's torso was parallel with the floor, as if being fucked from the front and the back, hence the name spit roast. Mark opened his mouth and took the shot from her breasts, throwing his head back and swallowing the liquid.

"That's twenty bucks each," Katie said, standing up and collecting the empty tubes from Micha and Mark. They were too amazed at what transpired to be upset about the price of the shots. They took the money from their wallets, along with a tip, and placed the money on Katie's tray.

"Hope you boys will be here for a while, I enjoy doing two at once," she winked and walked away, her ass bouncing as she brought the tray back to the bar.

* * *

Mark sprinkled a line of fine white powder across the formidable length of his cock. The thing was like a baby's arm when flaccid, and it always impressed him when he found a woman who could handle it. He swiped his finger across a small section of the powder and brought it up to his nose, snorting the coke.

Amid an all-time great Coke high, he watched as Katie took a momentary break from licking the head of his cock to snort a rail off of his shaft.

She tossed her head back—"Fuck! That's good,"—as Micha kept pumping away at her from behind.

Mark wasn't sure if she was talking about the coke or the cock. Judging by her cries of pleasure, and the wet slapping noise Micha's balls made when bouncing off of her soaking wet pussy, he assumed the answer was both.

The meaty member between Mark's legs was throbbing, it ached, begging for release. If he didn't blow his load soon, his cock might explode. He grabbed the back of Katie's head and guided her eager mouth back where it belonged. She gobbled his tube steak as if it was the last meal she'd ever eat.

Katie handled the spit roast well, and Mark couldn't be more satisfied. She had no problem paying attention to the cock in her mouth while her snatch was pounded from behind, each thrust forcing his beef stick further down her throat. Katie was a real keeper.

His balls tingled, and a familiar ache spread from his scrotum to his stomach, until it built up in his shaft and Mark could hold back no longer. He threw his head back in ecstasy as warm jets of cum pumped from his cock. "Fuck, I'm coming," Mark said.

"Mmmhhmm," Katie mumbled as she worked the shaft with her hand and mouth, twisting her wrist as she slid up and down his member, and while she hadn't been able to fit the entirety of his penis in her mouth, she was doing a damn fine job of taking every last drop of nut that splattered against the back of her throat.

Micha tossed his head back and moaned. He attacked Katie's pussy with renewed vigor, quickening his pace, eager to reach the finish line.

Katie moaned as her orgasm took hold, racking her body with waves of pleasure. Her wet vagina gripped Micha's penis, her pulsating warmth pushing him over the edge. Micha kept pounding away, even after cumming, until Katie had a second orgasm.

The three of them collapsed in a sweaty heap of tangled flesh and bodily fluids.

"God damn, that was something special right there," Micha said in his thick Texas drawl, reaching for his cell phone. He unlocked the device and navigated to his email. A shit-eating grin enveloped his face. He was overjoyed. Marcus Simpson had emailed him out of the blue and was throwing some kind of weekend party at a cabin.

TEN
GYM WAR

The gym stunk like shit. Stagnant, humid air clouded the gym despite multiple large steel fans set to full blast. The fans circulated the stale, hot air around the small square room, not helping any. The oniony smell of B.O. permeated the air and clung to every surface. It set in and latched on. It was so bad that even spectators smelled as if they had gone twelve rounds on the heavy bag when they left the gym.

Paul Renfield glanced at the clock. Two minutes remained in the round, but he was fucking exhausted. He didn't think he could go two more seconds, never mind minutes. Sweat dripped profusely from his brow line into his eyes, making it difficult to see. The swelling around his right eye didn't help with that cause, either. He flicked a jab at his sparring partner's face as he circled around the ring, but it was a lazy jab and his opponent caught it with his lead glove and looped a right hand over his own left.

The blow landed flush on Paul's jaw. The headgear did little to minimize the force of the punch, and Paul's leg buckled but he did not go down. He shook his head, both to clear the stars, and to tell his opponent *you didn't hurt me*.

JOHN LYNCH

But everyone who boxed knew posturing like that was bull-shit. You can shake your head all you want, but it doesn't change the fact that you're getting your ass handed to you.

Tired and hurt, if Teddy Atlas were commentating this session, he might say Paul's legs looked like they were gone.

That assessment would be correct.

What had started off as a routine sparring session had escalated into a dick measuring contest, and both Paul and his opponent were throwing every shot with bad intentions. They had gone eight hard rounds—three more than they had intended on going—and had grown a bit of an audience. This was the type of sparring session that goes down in the history of a gym. The type of session that turns into a legend.

Paul wasn't so sure he wanted to be remembered like that, but if it was going to happen, he sure as shit didn't want to be remembered as the guy they woke up with smelling salts.

He needed to get this guy out of here. Two more minutes was out of the question. He needed to dig deep and knock this fucker out, sparring etiquette be damned.

Paul slipped his opponent's jab and returned with one of his own, catching the man in his bird-like beak, crunching the nose and sending blood flying as his head whipped backward.

His opponent stumbled. Paul sensed the man's weakness and knew he couldn't let up. If he allowed his opponent to recover, he might be the one on the floor looking up at the ceiling, and he refused to be the one they peeled off the canvas.

Paul stepped in and feinted a jab. His opponent, dazed and trying to not get knocked out, bit on the feint, keeping his gloves high and tight, leaving his midsection exposed and ripe for the taking. Paul dug deep, fighting through the exhaustion, and threw a combo Mike Tyson had brutalized opponents with. He put all of his strength into a right hook to the man's exposed ribcage, forcing him to lean forward. As quickly as the punch landed, Paul had brought the arm back and torqued his body once more, landing a vicious uppercut that crumpled his opponent like a sack of shit.

Paul didn't bother checking on the unconscious body lying at his feet. A bloodlust had kicked in and allowed him to emerge victorious, and although there was supposed to be fair play in boxing, especially sparring, Paul didn't see it that way. To him, it was combat all over again. He tried to keep a lid on it, but sometimes it was too difficult for him to control that bloodlust and he became a passenger in his own body, helpless to stop the violence. When that happened, someone usually wound up hurt.

Today, he was happy it wasn't him, although he worried they would kick him out of the gym for sparring too hard. It wouldn't be the first time he was banned from a boxing gym, and it probably wouldn't be the last, but he was running out of local gyms, and soon would have to drive a long way if he wanted to continue to glove-up.

He stumbled out of the ring, hardly staying up. The adrenaline that had been keeping him on his feet subsided, and now he felt as though he were going to pass out.

Using his teeth, he peeled the velcro off of his gloves and removed them, followed by his headgear. He dropped the equipment into his gym bag and spat the mouthpiece into the bag as well, too tired to put it in its case. Paul let his body collapse to the floor, finally allowing it some rest. He rummaged through his bag and grabbed his phone.

He had one notification.

An email from Marcus Simpson.

ELEVEN
SERGEANT FINGER

Once a Marine, always a Marine. A slogan? Organizational propaganda? At one time in his life, Staff Sergeant Dennis Finger would have agreed with that notion. After all, the average Marine spends their entire time in the Corps hating the fact that they signed the contract. Hell, even men that end up reenlisting at the end of their contracts often seem sour on the 'Corps. Of course, you get the "motivators", the real fucking hard charging devil dogs. The guys who eat, sleep, shit, and piss the United States Marine Corps, but those men are few. They were certified crazy. In fact, they made the average Marine look mentally stable, and if Finger was being honest, there was no such thing as a mentally stable Marine. You had to be absolutely fucked in the head to volunteer for that shit.

Now retired, Finger no longer believed it was indoctrinating bullshit. The Corps had broken him down and rebuilt him into the man he was today. There had been highs and lows, but he couldn't deny the fact that he missed the Marine Corps.

After twenty years as a leatherneck, Finger had gracefully

bowed out of his service to his country. He had been sick of the bullshit for a long time. For most of his career, if he was being honest. But after just a few short months of life as a civilian, Finger found himself with an eagle, globe, and anchor-shaped hole in his heart. He talked to recruiters; he called everyone he could think of, but they all said the same thing, there was no turning back at this point in the game. They had pushed his retirement paperwork through, and the Corps would not take him back.

For some time after realizing he would never again don the uniform, Finger spiraled into depression. He found solace in alcohol and drugs before checking into a rehab and taking back control of his life. Once clean, he again spoke with the local recruiters and although they told him yet again he could not cancel his retirement, they offered him an opportunity to work as a civilian consultant to the local Marine reserve unit.

The unit was full of Marines fresh out of boot camp and infantry training battalion, but lacked men with experience. Aside from Staff NCOs, the only men with any kind of experience were a pair of Marines who had done an MOS change from Military Police to the infantry, but neither of them had the experience necessary to train Marines on the weapon systems, nor combat experience to impart on the junior Marines. They'd have to step up and become leaders when they inevitably deployed, but in the meantime, the Marine Corps had a genuine need for a man with the training and experience Finger had.

So yeah, he now believed that old saying. They might not let him reenlist, but he was *still* a Marine, Goddamnit, and nobody could take that from him.

Finger sped along 95-South. Drill weekend was over for the reserve unit, which meant he was done consulting until next month. They needed more time. The unit was staring down the barrel of a combat deployment that promised to be a difficult undertaking for the Marines. They were deploying to one of the worst areas in Afghanistan. This was not a deployment that should be given to a unit of nothing but weekend warriors. The one weekend a month training meant that despite knowing their jobs, the men would never be sharp. They would never be ready to fight the way an active duty unit would be. As admirable as their service to their country was, when you *played* Marine on the weekend you couldn't be expected to have that same edge.

Knowing they were fucked and he was the best chance they had at staying safe, Finger did his best to train them. He did his best to impart his twenty years of training, wisdom, and experience upon the Marines. These guys had the chips stacked against them already. Finger would be damned if he would not do his best to level the playing field for them.

With his mind already preoccupied with concocting new training exercises for next month's drill, Finger snapped to the present after his phone pinged with a new notification. Looking at it, he swerved and almost lost control of his Mustang. He let his foot ease off the gas until he achieved a reasonable traveling speed. With the vehicle once again under control, and traveling at a legal speed, Finger flicked the screen awake on his dashboard-mounted cell phone.

It was an email notification from Marcus Simpson.

Finger couldn't believe his eyes. He read through the email, reckless driving laws be damned. The boys were getting together, and Simpson had extended him an invitation.

At first, it surprised him to receive such an invitation, but when he let it stew in his mind, he realized it wasn't much of a shocker. Despite outranking all the men who would go, he had bonded with them in a way that was frowned upon by the senior leadership. Of course, they were brothers in combat, but there was more there. He drank with them, fraternized with them. Hell, he'd even been to the dingy strip clubs and nailed a few prostitutes with them occasionally, and in his twenty years of service, it was the tightest bond of brotherhood with any group of Marines he had ever experienced. There had been nothing like it before and nothing like it since.

Finger wasted no time in sending a reply. He hit compose on the email app and began tapping away at the virtual keyboard. Preoccupied and excited, he veered into the lane next to his. A horn beeped, and Finger looked up, correcting his course at the last moment. He damn near shit himself as he realized he had almost cut off an eighteen-wheeler, whose bumper had been right on his ass. He had come within a cunt hair of being turned into a red smear on the highway.

Finger took the next exit, pulled his car over, and finished replying to the email.

TWELVE
FATHER AND SON

"Thanks, Dad," Anthony said to Marcus. "I love the shakes here. I'm glad you changed your mind."

Marcus nodded his head, smiling at his son. "No problem, kiddo. You know I can't say no to you." He took another bite of his cheeseburger and realized he was telling the truth. He couldn't refuse the kid. Anthony had his father wrapped around his finger, and both father and son were well aware of that fact.

Marcus looked around the food court, taking in his surroundings. He sat with his back to the wall, observing everyone as they walked by. He took a mental note of everyone who entered the newly constructed Johnny Rockets. The place only had one point of entry and exit, but the floor to ceiling windows meant he had to monitor those, too.

Simpson couldn't help it, the constant surveying of his surroundings. When he had arrived at his duty station in Hawaii what seemed like a lifetime ago, one of the first nuggets of wisdom that his fellow Marines with combat experience had bestowed upon him was that after he had experienced war—in the flesh, not the glorification of it in

Hollywood—after he had lived, breathed, ate, shit, and pissed in a war zone every day month after month with the constant, smothering shadow of impending death around every corner, he would come home, if he was one of the lucky ones, a changed man. Paranoia of his fellow man would rule over him, and he would watch points of egress like a hawk. Sitting with his back to a wall would become a necessity, not a choice. How else would he make sure that nobody snuck up on him? And they were right. No matter how much work he put into healing himself, fixing whatever the war had broken within him, the urge to catalog every living being in his general vicinity, and have a plan to kill them if necessary, was something that would not be denied.

When you got down to the nitty gritty, the mall wasn't an ideal place for a man like Marcus Simpson. Too many anonymous faces in a sea of people. And this being America, any of those fish in the sea could pack enough heat to execute every Tom, Dick, and Harry in the immediate vicinity.

But despite how much he hated the anxiety-ridden experience of being in a crowded location, he hated disappointing Anthony even more. And so the father and son duo found themselves out for a day filled with greasy burgers, dairy infused obesity, and fries littered with enough salt to send his blood pressure through the roof. Just the way he liked it.

He had to admit, Oreo milkshakes sweetened the deal.

"What do you say we go to Dave and Busters and play some games after you finish that shake, tough guy?" Marcus sucked the dregs of his shake from the bottom of the glass, slamming it down harder than he meant to. He smiled as Anthony tried emulating his actions.

"I'll show you a tough guy on the Rockem' Sockem' Robots. I kicked your ass last time, Dad!"

"Keep running that mouth and I'm not gonna to let you win anymore."

"Like you could really beat me, Dad. You suck at games."

"Where did you get that mouth from? Maybe you were the Marine, not me." Marcus laughed and cuffed the back of Anthony's head. He threw a few bills on the table—enough to cover the food and the tip—then grabbed his phone and walked through the crowd with his son.

Hand in hand, father and son navigated the sea of people. While Anthony glanced around the mall, looking at all the different stores in amazement, no doubt searching for the perfect toy, Marcus committed the faces in the crowd to memory, and tried working out who and where trouble might come from.

They stepped on the escalators, making their slow ascension to the very top of the mall, a section made up of only two establishments. Dave and Busters and a movie theater.

"Daddy, Daddy! Can we go see a movie after Dave and Busters? The new Spider-Man movie is out!" Anthony tugged on Marcus's arm, his excitement showing in both his voice, and how he threatened to rip his father's arm clean off.

"Damn, kid, relax," Marcus laughed. "Why don't we check out the arcade first. The next showing isn't for a while. If we get out of here and the timing is right, *and* if you've been well behaved by the time we leave, then *maybe* we can go see the movie."

Marcus had been planning on taking Anthony to see the movie anyway, but he didn't tell that to his son. It was better to let the prospect of a movie dangle over the child's head. In Marcus's experience, a bit of bribery went a long way toward keeping children off the path of misbehavior, at least in the short term.

But Marcus was no psychologist. The Marine Corps had

turned him into a trained killer, and when he had been unceremoniously sent home he had tried to segue into a new position, one as a family man. Despite being a bona fide war hero, Marcus considered himself a failure. His marriage had failed. He had failed to save many of his friends overseas, and most recently, he had failed to check on his old squad mate, Eric Torres. He would not fail Anthony.

The loss of Eric Torres deeply saddened Marcus. Hell, Torres had even RSVP'd to the trip, and had talked about how excited he was at the prospect of seeing everyone again. Had he been lying? Marcus had no idea that his friend had been having such a rough go. To the best of his knowledge, losing Torres came as a surprise even to the men with whom he kept in regular contact. Whether Torres had shown signs or everyone had been ignorant to them, he couldn't say.

* * *

The father and son duo walked out of the movie theater fat and happy. If the milkshakes had filled them up, then the popcorn, candy, and soda had left them ready to burst. They both enjoyed the movie, Anthony more so than his father. Marcus was a bit of a web-head snob, and wasn't a fan of the character arc in this particular incarnation of the character, but he would take what he could get.

They made their way through the mall, taking far more time than necessary to get to the parking garage. All the stores were closed so there would be no more shopping, but Marcus was not ready to drop Anthony off. Normally, Anthony would have complained about the snail's pace, but tonight, his little body was exhausted. Tuckered out from all the junk food, video games, and late night at the movie theater.

When they reached the parking lot, the two hopped in the car and wound through the garage. Anthony was asleep before they had even made it to the highway.

Marcus's phone chirped.

The caller ID displayed the call as coming from the Department of Corrections.

That's weird. I don't know anyone locked up right now.

Marcus looked over at Anthony sleeping in the passenger seat. He didn't want to wake his son, but he had a feeling this call was important.

He answered the call and turned the bluetooth functionality off before anyone spoke. A call coming through the speaker might wake Anthony.

"Hello?"

Static on the other line before a voice finally broke the silence. "Marcus, it's me. I fucked up. I need help."

Marcus continued driving, deftly navigating with one hand on the wheel and the other holding the phone in place against his ear. "Huggies?" he asked. "I'm listening. What do you need from me?"

THIRTEEN
BAIL

F rom Saturday evening until Monday evening, Ray sat in the state's only jail. Bobby had stuck around after Ray fled the scene of the fight, giving a witness statement to the responding officers. He had told them he hadn't seen shit, but the cops weren't buying it. After throwing him in the back of a cruiser and threatening to search his vehicle, Bobby had told the cops about the fight, but had not mentioned Ray's name. The cops put out an APB and immediately canvased the neighborhood. The brutality of what Ray had done to the man outside the bar looked very little like self-defense to the responding officers, and they wanted to find the man responsible.

A brief search around the neighborhood had ensued, and Ray hid behind a patch of bushes on someone's front lawn, but a passing patrol car had trained its spotlight on the exact location Ray had hunkered down. As it turned out, since he dwarfed the bushes, trying to hide in them wasn't exactly the best course of action. Ray had been drunk off his ass, and if the hiding spot he selected hadn't proved that he wasn't

97

thinking clearly, the life-threatening ass-whooping he dished out sure as hell did.

Although he was housed alone in a cell within the unit they assigned him to, the accommodations were far from adequate. The tattered mattress had clearly seen better days. Ray refused to sleep on it, for fear of scabies. Instead, he slept on the small chair welded to the writing desk that was welded to the cell's wall. The entire place stunk like urine and shit, and the officers had refused to let him clean his cell. They thought it was funny to let him sit in filth. Clearly, the inmate that had been housed there before him had been disgusting, and Ray felt grimy by the simple act of standing in the cell. The officer told him that since the judge granted him bail, they would not allow him to clean the cell. What was the point if he could leave as soon as someone posted the bail. If he didn't like that, well then they told him he was welcome eat a face full of pepper spray and move to solitary confinement.

The officer in question, Roderick, was a dickhead, a tiny runt of a man that Ray could easily snap in half if he was so inclined, but the prospect of adding a few years for assaulting an officer of the law to whatever sentence he may face for the assault outside of the bar was enough to stay his temper—for the time being.

The sound of watery shit splashing the toilet in the cell next to his broke the early morning silence. The stench of shit traveled through the vent between Ray's cell and the man evacuating his bowels next door. It overpowered the area's normal scent of piss and body odor, and for a moment Ray thought he might vomit.

He held his breath, barely keeping the contents of his stomach inside of his body. "Jesus Christ, man," Ray called out. "I think you need to go to medical. Something died inside your asshole. That's fucking rank."

"I can't help it, big dog. You know what those spicy chicken patties they gave us for dinner last night do to a man," his neighbor said.

The two men shared a laugh at that. Ray kept to himself, mostly, and didn't know the fellow next door's name, but he got along with the guy just fine.

"Whoop whoop," a voice from somewhere within the cell block echoed.

Whenever an officer entered the area, someone would give the signal. It wasn't uncommon to hear numerous toilets flushing at that point, a last ditch effort to get rid of whatever drugs or contraband an inmate didn't want to get caught with. Ray didn't bother with shit like that, and although he'd kill for a cigarette, he didn't feel like going to segregation over it. Besides, around here, the only way to get cigarettes back to the block was to "cheek them," and Ray didn't feel like smoking a cigarette that had been smuggled inside another man's ass.

The sound of the officer's boots striking the floor echoed throughout the area, and aside from his footfalls and the jingling of his over-large keyset, the block was so quiet if you listened close enough you could hear a mouse fart. Ray, along with the rest of the inmate population in that housing area, knew that when officer Roderick came around, you stood up and kept your mouth shut. The man might be a tiny, sniveling turd of a human, but he would still fuck your cell up, leaving you to clean up the tornado that had gone through it when you went to chow or rec or any other area you might have gone to throughout the day.

The footfalls grew louder as Roderick made his way closer to Ray's cell, before halting.

Shit.

Ray turned and looked through the narrow window in the center of his cell door. He didn't see anyone, but as he was about to sit down, Officer Roderick banged on his cell door with his baton.

"Hey, fuckface," Officer Roderick said.

Ray didn't respond, he would not be goaded into a pissing match with the staff around here. He didn't need that kind of headache, and, frankly, he surprised himself with the way he had kept his anger in check these past few days. Ray was afraid that if he engaged with the officer, he might do something stupid.

Roderick stared at Ray, the simmering anger visible in his eyes. "Pack your shit up. Someone must love you. They bailed your stupid ass out a few hours after you returned from court."

Ray smiled and walked to the cell door. "I knew you were my favorite, Officer Roderick."

"Don't worry, you'll be seeing me again, I'm sure. This place is a revolving door for you people."

"You people? I'm not a fucking criminal. I got into a fight."

"Yeah, nobody here is a criminal, Hughes. I bet you're innocent, just like everyone else around here. Just pack your shit up and get the fuck out. If you want to take your sweet ass time, we can postpone your release until tomorrow. It would be a shame if I found some drugs in your cell when you left."

The implied threat was enough to convince Ray to stop fucking around with Officer Roderick and be on his merry way. He picked up the few belongings that he had acquired over the weekend and exited the cell block, hopefully for the last time. Ray knew he was about to get an earful from

Marcus Simpson about an entire laundry list of things. Maybe staying behind bars would be better after all.

Officer Roderick grabbed a crumpled piece of paper from the floor, unfolded it, and read the sloppy handwriting.

* * *

I've fucked up, yet again. This time, I'm not so sure I'm going to escape with my freedom. But maybe I don't deserve freedom. I just don't know anymore. I'm a wreck. I can't sleep, hardly eat. I don't take care of myself. I keep having these nightmares about a woman we accidentally killed in Iraq. I've had nightmares every single day for the last five years. The VA has had me on all sorts of meds. I've been on so many antidepressants, I couldn't even name them all to you. Sleeping pills, anti-anxiety pills, blood pressure pills, pills to suppress the nightmares. None of it works. It's like I have two default settings. Emotionless robot, and hot-headed psychopath. Oh, and depressed. So I guess that makes three settings. I've done group therapy, one-on-one therapy. I've seen psychologists, psychiatrists. Nobody can help me. Always, I see her.

So I stopped taking the meds. If I can't stop seeing her, I don't want to take a bunch of pills that make me feel like shit. I drive little these days. If the nightmares weren't enough, I keep having flashbacks. They come out of nowhere. At first, it seemed driving in traffic triggered them, but after a few months, there is no rhyme or reason. They just happen. I think it has something to do with the woman we killed. I don't think it's a nightmare. If it was, why don't the pills work? The doctors told me it's sleep paralysis, but that's bullshit. I know what I'm seeing, and it pisses me off when those pencil-pushing bureaucrats at the VA treat me like a guinea pig and *write-off what is happening to me as if it's just some kind of hallucination. It's not. I know what I'm seeing.*

I kind of hope the judge doesn't let me out. I almost killed a man. I don't know why I did it. The guy was annoying, and a bigot, but I could have just walked away. I didn't though. I'm in here and he's in the hospital.

I wish this would stop.

FOURTEEN
AN ULTIMATUM

"No way, I'm not fucking doing it." Ray stared out the passenger side window, refusing to make eye contact with Marcus.

Marcus kept both hands on the wheel as they came around a bend on the highway. He drummed his fingers on the steering wheel, using the repetitive motion as a method to calm his own agitation at Ray's stubbornness.

"You're going, Ray. We need this. *You* need this. It will be good to get everyone back together, talk shit out in a setting that isn't just clinical VA bullshit."

Ray whipped his head in Marcus's direction. "Listen, Simpson, maybe you didn't hear me. I'm not going. I don't want to see the guys. I don't give a fuck about meeting up with anyone. I want to forget I was a Marine. I don't want to reminisce in some bullshit, macho circle jerk session with a bunch of type-A assholes who can't get over the fact that we're civilians now, and nobody gives a fuck about us."

Marcus inhaled, taking time to think over what Ray said. It was a lot to unpack, and Marcus felt his blood pressure rising. That old hothead in him was still there, and he was getting ready to make his big comeback and unload on Ray.

"No, you listen to me, motherfucker. You don't know the hoops I just had to jump through, the calls I had to make, the favors I had to pull with everyone from the VA to the local police department just to get the judge to let you out on bail." Marcus eased off the gas and coasted, turning to look at Ray while he spoke. "Part of the condition of your bail agreement is that you attend the retreat. I pitched it as an intense weekend of in-patient therapy treatment. Almost like a drug rehab program. Make no mistake, brother, you need help. You know Torres suck-started his fucking AR, right? You want to end up like that? Do you wanna end up killing the next guy who pisses you off because the drugs the VA pedals can't keep your shit under control, so you self-medicate and act like you're ok? You can't sleep, you can't eat, so all you do is drink. Does that sound familiar?"

Ray didn't respond. He kept silent, staring out the windshield. Marcus couldn't tell if he was listening, or staring off into space.

"I hit the nail on the head, right?" Marcus asked. "I know I did, because you're not the only one going through this shit. This is what I do. I help the guys that are too fucked up to know that their fuse is running dangerously short, and the shit is about to explode." Marcus didn't tell him that Officer Roderick showed him the note he found in the cell after Ray left.

Ray looked at Marcus.

He was listening.

Marcus pressed on, hoping he would choose the only reasonable option. Spend the weekend at the retreat. The healing process was going to hurt, but would Ray really rather go to jail than get his shit together? "A bunch of the guys are going man, you need this, and I need to help you. I couldn't help Torres. Please, let me help you."

The floodgates opened ever so slightly as tears welled up in Marcus's eyes. He tried to keep them in check. Tried to keep from a full on breakdown, and while he was successful at avoiding a meltdown, the pain and hurt of losing Torres was too much to hide all emotion, no matter how much he wanted to keep it together in front of Ray.

Maybe showing some vulnerability would convince Ray he wasn't alone, and he didn't have to keep his demons to himself.

"Ok, I'll do it," Ray said. "But if I don't like what's going on, if I decide I don't want to be there, I'm out. And after this weekend, I want to be left alone. You have *no idea* what I'm going through. It's not in some bullshit social worker manual. There are no tips and tricks for what's wrong with me. I'm not doing it for you, or for Torres. I'm not even doing it because I fucked that man up outside of the bar. I'm doing it so I don't have to sit in a prison cell."

Marcus didn't care for that attitude, but it was a foot in the door. In Marcus's time doing social work and veterans outreach, everyone thought their situation was unique. They thought that because the specifics of what they had gone through were different, that nobody could know what they were experiencing. Often, it was an attitude that could be worked through, with some time and effort.

Marcus hoped one weekend together would provide adequate time to find the weak point in Ray's self-erected defense mechanisms, although he feared it would not be. PTSD survivors didn't spend years constructing walls and defenses for them to topple at the first push.

For the time being, this weekend would have at least one minor victory—it kept Ray out of jail, at least while he had charges pending. The judge had agreed to let him out on bail, with the stipulation that Ray attend this retreat, but with no significant progress extending past this upcoming weekend Marcus wasn't so sure he could keep Ray out of prison no matter how many favors he called in and strings he pulled.

But if Marcus could get through to Ray, convince him to take his mental health seriously, and maybe even get him going to therapy, there was a chance, albeit a small one, that the judge would take Ray's service record into consideration and grant probation rather than prison time.

Marcus continued driving along the highway, glancing once more at Ray, who clearly looked as if he was having trouble keeping his cool.

At first, Simpson thought this weekend would be a blast once they got the heavy shit out of the way. Now, it promised to be long and arduous.

Simpson felt a migraine coming on.

FIFTEEN

THE BOYS ARE BACK IN TOWN

After a long, drawn out week of keeping tabs on Ray, Marcus was *almost* satisfied they would get through the week without another incident. Friday arrived, and it was time to get the show on the road.

Initially, the plan was to pick everyone up from the airport as they flew in, dropping them off at the cabin, leaving them unattended while he and Ray picked the next arrival up. It didn't take Marcus long to realize what a horrible idea that was. He spent a few moments playing the scenarios out in his head, and most of them ended with the cabin up in flames. The only actual way to keep these clowns out of trouble was to babysit them. That had been true even *before* they had all suffered through traumatic experiences in the Marine Corps. They were always rowdy, substance-abusing party animals, and for some of them, that hadn't changed. The only difference between then and now was time, injuries, and an average of thirty pounds of added weight.

Knowing that many of them had issues, and having zero trust they *wouldn't* wreck the place, Simpson decided they would *all* play chauffeur today. If Simpson learned one thing in the Corps, it was that babysitting these guys was the only way to keep them in check.

With the last of the crazy bastards in the back of the minivan, Simpson felt like a soccer mom driving around the world's worst behaved children. The gang was back together, minus those who lost their lives overseas, and those who lost their lives in the war at home. Marcus knew he would never stop veteran suicide, but maybe with some luck, he could prevent it from hitting so close to home again.

Everyone was in the minivan now. The last stop had been swinging back around to pick up Ray, who had spent the day playing Call of Duty in Marcus's apartment while Simpson played his best rendition of an Uber driver.

"Hey, Marcus, let's stop at the bar and get some wings and some drinks," Micha called from the back of the van.

"I could go for some wings. PJ's has great wings. It's just too bad it's not Monday; they do a wing night fifty cents a wing," Marcus said.

"Do they sell the boneless ones?" Paul asked.

Mark laughed, adding his two cents. "Is that where Ray beat the brakes off that dickhead?"

Ray turned around in his seat. "Keep it up and you're next, fuckface."

Marcus wasn't sure if the ball-busting was the guys falling back into old routines, or if tensions were running high. It was hard to gauge it, and Simpson considered jumping in.

He didn't have to. Finger had the same idea. "Why don't we relax a bit guys, lay off each other's dicks for a few minutes. Maybe give one another time to adjust?"

Mark erupted in laughter again. "Finger, are you fucking with us right now? Why don't *you* lay off *my* dick, so your sister has room to fit. Besides, Huggies knows I'm just busting his balls."

Haney shook his head. "You assholes haven't changed a bit, huh?"

Simpson paid close attention to the exchange and tried to catch facial expressions in from his rearview. He still couldn't tell who was joking and who was not. Either way, one thing was for sure, the comment about Ray's case had went straight up his ass. You could practically see the steam coming off of Ray's forehead.

Maybe a night out for drinks before heading to the cabin would help everyone blow off steam.

"Fuck PJ's," Ray said. "He wants to see the bloodstains where I stomped numbnuts out, so let's go to The Frosted Thug."

The peanut gallery in the back all chimed in, pleasantries such as "Fuck yeah" and "Stomp another asshole out." Marcus thought that if he took these guy's anywhere other than The Frosted Thug, *he* might be the one getting stomped out tonight.

* * *

Melonie was there, thank God for that. If Ray was going to be forced into a night out with these assholes, he thought he should at least be afforded some eye candy. And God damn if Mel wasn't looking like a snack tonight.

She almost threw them out before they had even taken their seats at one of the two tables they had shoved together in the bar's corner. Mel had mentioned something about her boss not wanting trouble, and him having an issue with patrons killing each other outside of the bar. She wasn't serious though and had every intention of letting them in. Her boss might not want Ray there, but her boss wasn't working at the moment, and Ray knew she would not pass up on the opportunity for the large amount of tips a group of drunken former Marines was liable to leave.

In the minds of his friends, Ray had an aura of mystery surrounding him. Due in large part to the fact that he never kept in touch with anyone, but every once in a while, a rumor got out about how Ray was doing, his run-ins with the law. Some rumors were true, some unfounded, but his pending assault charge went a long way toward reinforcing the picture they had already painted in their minds.

Ray didn't give two shits. He had no time for anyone, not when he was on the cusp of losing himself.

Not when *she* visits him in his sleep every night. He had told none of the other guy's about it. Only Simpson, and even then, he only spilled the beans because Simpson eventually told him about the note they found in his cell.

All the pills in the VA pharmacy couldn't erase her. The revolving door of mental health doctors didn't believe him, and none of them stuck around at the VA long enough to really get to know him. To learn he wasn't a liar. To learn that he was a human being, not a living, breathing trauma to solve. Simpson was just like them, and Ray wished he had said nothing.

They told him it was just guilt. Nightmares bleeding into bouts of sleep paralysis. But they didn't see her. He did.

In the blackest moments of the night, she was there. Ripped from his sleep like a newborn slipping out of the birth canal, he saw things that shouldn't be. She was dead, but the dead of night gave new life to the horrors of the world. Each time she manifested and left him paralyzed he welcomed death, but she failed to deliver. Instead, tormenting him, dangling the sweet respite that only the grave could provide like a piece of bacon in front of a begging dog. He had taken her life, accidentally. She saw to it that he *wished* she would return the favor.

That was how he knew she was real. How could a flashback leave him paralyzed, and torture him so, even if it was only temporary? Sleep Paralysis? Those quacks could get their faces fucked.

* * *

As the drinks flowed, everyone in the party relaxed and fit into their old roles. Liquid courage, their old friend, also doubled as liquid comfortability. Simpson benefited most from this new found comfort, relaxing just enough that his up-tight ass eased the death grip it had on the stick that had seemed lodged in it until recently. He had been worrying so much about the mental health of everyone, treating his friends as if he were their therapist, that he had forgotten what he really was—a concerned friend who was in a profession that allowed him to help them.

Despite the relaxed demeanor of the Marines, Simpson couldn't help but notice Ray seemed a bit off. The man clearly wasn't doing well. He talked as if everything was fine, and even downplayed his current legal situation, but Simpson knew better. Ray gave off the vibes of a man who was stuck in the darkness of his own mind, but was too proud to ask for help.

That was a problem that troubled most men. The stigma that talking about their problems, and their well-being was a sign of weakness. Societal norms placed this burden on men, and the problem became much worse when you looked at men in certain professions, military men and veterans especially. Since the day you put your feet on the yellow foot-prints at Parris Island, you're told that you're weak, both mentally and physically, and you must always be stronger. You're told that when you're hurt, you can always push through, because if you can't then you're just being a pussy.

The result of such training is a fighting force of men and women who are told that even in times of pain and vulnerability, they must never show it. It becomes embedded in their psyche. The Marine Corps gloats about breaking recruits down in order to build them up, a task the Corps manages expertly, for how else would you go about training men and women to become literal killing machines? A side effect of this rewiring of the brain, one that is not talked about openly, is that most of the men and women who've undergone this transformation and are lucky enough to come home, do so only to find out they've been changed irrevocably and struggle through much of their lives, trying to find humanity inside of the robotic husk of who they have become.

Simpson motioned for their server. "Miss, can I get four Bud Lights and two Jager bombs please?"

Melonie walked away and returned a few minutes later, balancing a tray full of drinks on one hand. "Who's drinking what?" she asked.

"Two buds for myself, and two for him," he said, motioning at Ray. "And one shot a piece."

She looked annoyed. "Listen, if your buddy here beats the shit out of someone again, I'm going to lose my job. He's not supposed to be here. You guys better leave a damn good tip, because I'm risking my ass here."

Simpson smiled at her. "He won't be fighting anyone tonight. I'll beat his ass myself if he tries."

The server sucked her teeth for a moment, contemplating

her options. In the end, she gave the two men their drinks, as Simpson had expected all along.

"Don't make me regret this," she said, walking away from the table.

"Marcus, you really want to do this?" Ray nodded at the drinks in front of them?

Marcus's smile illuminated his entire face. "Every good time we've ever had started with a bad idea, right? Besides, with all of us here, nothing is going to happen. We will have a few more drinks and then head out."

Ray didn't respond; he simply chugged the first Bud Light and chased it with the Jager Bomb before sipping on the last beer.

Simpson wasn't sure whether or not they were headed in the right direction, but he mirrored Ray's actions as the two men recreated their old drinking ritual. It seemed to Simpson that even old, dead habits can be dug up from the grave.

SIXTEEN
THE CABIN

Although the cabin Simpson secured for the weekend was a short distance from the bar the boy's had closed out, it had taken them some time to make the drive. Simpson, despite knowing better, had not assigned a designated driver, and rather than call multiple Uber's, he drove drunk, making his way slowly to the cabin, trying to not do anything to get pulled over.

It was late, and there weren't many vehicles on the road, nor did they seem to pass by many signs of civilization. While they weren't far from shopping centers, or other places where one would expect to see people, they had to take quite a few side roads through the woods to get to the cabin. There wasn't much else out this way, and the narrow roads reflected that.

The van traveled along the winding dirt road for what seemed to Simpson like ages, and he caught himself driving too fast more than once. He needed to keep his speed in check. A DUI this weekend wouldn't be good for anyone.

The cabin sat on a large plot of land and was the only piece of property around for acres. Hiking trails, shooting ranges, and plenty of surrounding woods for hunting would provide the men with ample opportunity to let some steam off and talk their shit out.

There was even a trail that wound through the woods for about a mile before ending at a large pond. The pond itself wasn't actually private, but there were no other properties on the cabin's side of the pond, and no other way to get to the pond from that side. When renting the weekend, the property manager had told Simpson the oversized storage area would have kayaks, rowboats, paddleboats, and other outdoor sporting equipment.

One thing was certain, they wouldn't be at a loss for things to do this weekend.

Simpson brought the van to a halt, doing a three-point turn in the driveway, and backing up as close to the cabin as possible. The shorter the distance for everyone to drunkenly stumble through the doors the better.

The men hopped out one by one, stretching their legs and yawning. Mark leaned over and vomited in the driveway, making no attempt to vomit away from the cabin.

"You're cleaning that up, asshole," Finger said, slapping Mark in the back.

The impact rattled Mark's stomach enough to forcefully eject more of its contents into the gravel.

A few of the guys dry-heaved at the stench of Mark's vomit, which somehow overpowered the pine trees surrounding them. Mark stood up and wiped his mouth off. He stretched and peeled his sweaty, vomit stained top off of his body. The cool, night breeze was a welcome change from the hot bar and stuffy van ride.

"I remember my first beer," Simpson said. "Now if you ladies are done throwing up, we can unpack the van and check out the accommodations."

Haney put his arm around Simpson's shoulders. "Man, I didn't realize this place would be in the middle of nowhere. I mean, you said it was in the woods, but it's Rhode Island, I thought for sure you were just exaggerating."

Paul grabbed his suitcase from the rear of the van. "Can we see Quahog before my plane ride out of here?"

Ray looked at Paul, clearly stupefied by the question. Simpson laughed. "Not an actual place, numbnuts. Try looking at a fucking map once in a while." Simpson couldn't believe it. These morons had been asking him about a fictional town from a fucking cartoon for years, and these crayon-eating assholes were too stupid to realize it.

"It's a sausage fest here. I hope we run across some bitches at the pond," Micha said.

Simpson shook his head. "First off, this side of the pond is private. Nobody will be there but us. Second, bitches? Are you fifteen, Micha? Good to see you're still the same dumbass you've always been."

"Dude, it's a joke."

Simpson didn't dignify that with a response. Some guys were incapable of change. They were here to work through mental issues. If Micha had misogynistic issues to work through, and he did, he would have to reach out to someone else. Micha was the type of guy that Simpson only tolerated because of what they'd been through together. And it didn't hurt that living in the barracks back in the day was like living in the world's biggest frat house. But now? Simpson had no tolerance for guys like that. He was a better man than that, and was raising a boy to become a better man than that. Marcus couldn't help but think about the ass whooping he'd have to give his son if he ever caught him talking about a woman that way.

Everyone gathered at the back of the van and shot the shit

117

while waiting their turn to grab their bags. Besides his suit-case, Micha, in all his southern redneck glory, had shipped his AR-15. God forbid he went on a trip without it. Simpson didn't see what the point of it was, they had hunting rifles at the cabin to use for target practice, but a redneck is going to redneck.

With the van unloaded, they made their way into the cabin.

The warrior retreat was now underway.

PART THREE
THE END OF THE WAR

SEVENTEEN
THE GOOD TIMES ROLL ON

Although they had closed the bar out and taken their time traveling to the cabin, none of the men were ready for bed yet. Marcus loaded the refrigerator with beer and laid the collection of alcohol along the bar counter. Luckily, he had the foresight to get alcohol before picking everyone up from the airport.

The cabin had to be one of the nicest places he had ever stayed. The sprawling acreage, every in-suite amenity you could ask for, the recreational opportunities on the property. All on the dime of a wonderful veteran non-profit. Simpson's work with veterans had introduced him to many contacts within various agencies, departments, and organizations. It was enough that when he needed to get help for someone, he likely had the resources to get it.

Simpson had known other Marines who booked retreats such as this one, and so he thought he would pitch it to the Leathernecks for Leathernecks fund. He wasn't sure what to expect, but within a week of the first email he had sent to the company, they had already organized a list of locations and dates for him to choose from. Leathernecks for Leathernecks covered all expenses, including travel fees for those who couldn't afford them.

T he lack of daylight did little to lower the temperature —July through early September in Rhode Island was typically brutal with sweltering heat and humidity that made you feel as if you were walking through a jungle. Despite the weather, they sat around the fireplace, shooting the shit and keeping the alcohol train rolling. The ambience was too perfect to *not* get a fire going. The log cabin aesthetic and modern sensibilities met in the middle for an experience that was nothing less than picturesque.

Haney reached into his backpack and pulled out two joints. Simpson wasn't sure where those had come from. He assumed Haney must have bought them from someone at the bar; he didn't think Haney had somehow smuggled them on the plane. No way he was that stupid.

Simpson opened his mouth to say something to Haney about the weed, but thought better of it and let the words die in his throat. Marijuana wasn't the problem. Yes, these guys all had varying degrees of substance abuse issues, but Simpson didn't believe marijuana to be the gateway drug that anti-drug campaigns labeled it. The only gateway he saw in marijuana was that it stood to reason that if a guy can get you weed, he could probably get you harder shit, or at least point you in the direction. And While the VA doesn't prescribe medical marijuana as a treatment for PTSD, Simpson knew many Marines who benefited from its use, and the results were irrefutable, no matter what opponents of legalization may claim.

Micha looked Ray up and down. "Hey man, when did you get all tatted up like that?" he asked.

Ray looked down at his own arms. Tattooless when he had last seen his friends; full sleeves now covered both of his arms. Dragons, skulls, graveyards, grim reapers. He had a bit of everything, and he had allowed his body to become a canvas for one of his favorite local tattoo artists. All black and gray of course. His last piece was to be a leg sleeve. It was going to be a horror movie sleeve, filled with various slasher icons. If he didn't end up in prison, he hoped to start the sleeve soon. After that, about the only free skin he had left on his massive frame was between his legs, and he didn't intend to get that particular organ done.

"I've been getting them done for a few years now, ever since coming home. I don't have much else to spend my money on,"

Micha laughed. "Nothing to spend your money on? That's a thing?" He kept badgering Ray. "Seriously, are you a hobo or something? You look like shit, if I'm being honest."

Ray chewed his lip.

Simpson didn't think Ray wanted to indulge Micha in conversation at the moment. He still seemed a bit pissed off from the ride to the cabin, and Micha was clearly pushing buttons. He'd been trying to get a rise out of everyone all night. Some people never grew up.

"Micha, you're going to want to shut the fuck up. I'm sick of you already, and you're one stupid comment away from getting skull fucked," Ray said, standing up.

Micha, clearly intimidated, tried to throw water on the fire he had been stoking all evening. "Relax man, I'm busting your balls."

The two joints made their way around the circle of Marines in opposite directions, as soon as they passed one, another was in their hand ready to go. In a matter of minutes they were wrecked. Finger was passed out on the floor and

Mark and Paul were struggling to keep their eyes open. Micha stumbled around the room telling perverted jokes, as everyone expected of him. Only Simpson, Ray, and Haney seemed to keep their shit together.

Simpson stood up, chugging the last of his beer. "Guy's, I'm glad we all got together to do this. Thank you for being here. Seriously. I know you're probably wondering why we're all getting wasted and smoking pot on a trip like this, and I get that, but the problems are deeper than drinking and weed. Some of you need to limit the alcohol, sure, and if that's you, I'm going to get you where you need to be. But I'm more concerned about the harder shit and the mental issues we've all got going on."

"The VA tells me I've got plenty of issues," Haney chimed in.

"Fuck the VA!" Paul yelled. "They've got a pill for everything these days. They even have pills to cure the side effects of the pills they gave me to cure the other shit I've got going on. I get four free Viagra a month to cure the ED I got from the citalopram they gave me to unfuck my brain. Ain't that something special?"

"Yeah man, I know what you mean," Mark laughed, removing his prosthetic leg and holding it up in a mock salute, "I get laxatives prescribed to me for the constipation pain meds gave me."

"What's that like, walking around on that thing?" Haney asked.

Mark cracked open a beer and poured it into the hollow of the fake leg. He chugged the beer and wiped the foam from his lips when he was through. "Annoying, but it's better than the wheelchair I was in. At least this way, if I wear long pants nobody can tell anything is off about me, and I don't have to deal with the pity party stares and dirty looks everyone gives me. And you can do cool shit with it." Mark laughed, holding the leg out as an offer to anyone else who wanted to drink beer mixed with a bit of stump sweat. One hell of a concoction.

Simpson cleared his throat. "And that is why we are all here, because clearly everyone here needs help. You, Mark, you *definitely* need help." Simpson paused for a moment, and continued in a somber tone. "Torres needed help but nobody had his six."

For a moment, everyone sat in silence, remembering their fallen brother.

Not one to keep his mouth shut for long, Micha broke the silence. "Sit the fuck down!" he slurred. "Give us one day without the kumbaya circle-jerk shit, Marcus."

"Yeah, great Micha. I'm being serious here. We lost another one. Torres decided he wanted to suck start a rifle rather than get help. I promise you, nothing you're going through is so bad that you need to do that. Call me any time of the night, I don't care. You're not a pussy for reaching out. I'd rather listen to you all cry than have to hear it from your mothers at your funeral."

Tears escaped Simpson's eyes. He had held back the sobs, but it was only a matter of time before those broke free. Simpson had seen too much, had known too many men who were so ruined by the atrocities they saw, and the violence they had to commit overseas, that when they had finally come home, when they could place the rifle down and become the person they were destined to be, they found themselves tangled by the chains of their past.

Wiping the tears from his cheeks, Simpson tried to lighten the mood. "Now, I'm done with the kumbaya shit. You turds pack up and get some sleep. Tomorrow, we're going to have some fun," Simpson said. "Oh, and we are *definitely* doing more of these talks tomorrow, Micha. So be prepared."

"Yeah, I'll be sure to smoke some more of this shit before we do," Micha replied.

Simpson let the conversation end there. These guys needed help, he knew it, and they knew it. They would never admit as much; it went against everything that had been drilled into them in training, but deep down everyone knew the truth. They'd already walked miles in each other's boots, and they didn't need to guess what one another was going through.

The sun crept over the horizon, bringing the first rays of light along the lakeside. One by one, the men finished their drinks and turned in for the night.

Ray sat motionless on a reading nook built into the bay window frame, watching the sun seize control over the darkness.

Eventually, he turned in and attempted to sleep.

The Marines, the rest of his squad, slept like the dead.

EIGHTEEN
NIGHT TERRORS AND FLASHBACKS

T*he call for fire was complete. Ray Hughes and the rest of his squad rode through the desert. The heat was oppressive. A few days' worth of sand, dirt, and grime covered their skin. New, fresh sweat covered their bodies even as old, dried sweat left their clothing salt stained and crusty. Ray's socks, if removed from his feet, could probably stand on their own at this point, no foot necessary.*

One week of combat operations outside the wire. The mission had taken longer than expected, rations were running low, morale even lower. After days of no actionable intelligence, their platoons forward observer at last gave the men what they were waiting for. Insurgents had been seen moving through a local village, however, keeping civilians nearby at all times, ensuring that the Marine's hands were tied—the country had seen far too much unnecessary bloodshed. Hearts and minds was the current mission, collateral damage was to be avoided at all costs, as it should be, but that didn't change the fact that cowards hiding amongst women and children made it difficult to get the job done.

Eventually, the insurgents slipped up, at least enough

that the forward observer felt comfortable relaying grid coordinates for Ray and his gun team to drop round after round of 81MM steel rain. By the time the patrol made it to the scene of destruction to do a proper battle damage assessment, the grisly display stabbed Ray like a dagger in the heart.

Amongst the chaos and ruin, there was no sign of insurgent activity, but that didn't mean the rounds had whiffed. No, the rounds had been on target, but rather than enemy combatants, there was a catastrophic loss of civilian life. Chunks of bone, body parts, and viscera littered the ruins of the building. The forward observer's intelligence had been bad, and innocent men, women, and even children had all paid the price for his mistake.

Ray stared at what remained of a woman, bits and pieces of her ruined frame sticking out from the rubble. Blood and dust converged around her body, leaving a thick pool of congealing blood that took on a mud-like consistency. Her face was torn apart, the broken jaw repositioned to the opposite side of her face. Both of her legs were gone. Ragged holes and torn flesh revealed the meat and gristle underneath her skin. Pieces of internal organs, exposed and punctured by the shrapnel of repeated mortar rounds doing what they had been designed to do.

Maim and kill.

Ray vomited in the sand. Filthy chunks of partially digested cheese and veggie omelet MRE hit the ground, splattering on his boots and the corpse. The smell of death, blood, and vomit kept Ray dry heaving, even after the contents of his stomach were completely empty.

The acidic mixture from his digestive system further desecrated the corpse, and despite all the previous death and destruction, despite the desensitization and dehumanization, the last act of desecration Ray accidentally committed sent him on a downward spiral.

He cried. The stress, the fear, the horror of war seen daily finally tore down the last segment of the mental wall Ray had constructed within his mind, no longer allowing him to shrug off the atrocities and pretend there was anything normal about operating in a combat zone.

* * *

R ay shot up from his bed, a silent scream stuck in his throat. Sweat covered his body, permeating the room in a funk of body odor and alcohol. Tears fell from his cheeks as his chest heaved up and down, his heart racing, trying to punch a hole through his chest.

The surrounding room was blurry at the edges of his vision and he struggled to keep his breathing under control. Once again, he was plagued with night terrors of his past atrocities. The woman whose life he had erroneously taken always in his mind.

Flashes of her face assaulted him. One moment he saw the room around him, the next her face, pale and ruined, as she had appeared to him in his waking nightmare all those years ago in Iraq. She tormented him, and he knew that the nightmare overseas had not been a nightmare at all, but the beginning stages of a scorned specter out for revenge.

"Leave me alone!" Ray screamed.

He got up and crossed the room, but saw her in front of the door, blocking the exit.

Ray backpedaled, his heel catching the floor at an awkward angle, sending him flat on his ass. He scrambled backwards, trying to create space between himself and the apparition. He knew what his therapist would say: that he was dreaming, and that part of his brain was asleep, while the other part was awake, causing the dream to bleed into the real world. Nothing more than one part of the brain waking while the other still slept. They told him the same thing about what happened to him in Iraq. That there was never any dead woman. It was nothing more than sleep paralysis. He wasn't paralyzed now, and she was still here.

Bullshit.

She charged at him, coming closer at an impossible clip, stopping and appearing instantly closer, like a frozen image being fast forwarded.

Ray closed his eyes and screamed. His body trembled, and he waited for death to take him. When he finally stopped screaming, his throat sore and bloodied from screaming, he opened his eyes and there she was, their noses touching.

She let loose a high-pitched wail, and Ray blacked out.

NINETEEN
AWOL

The sun had risen long before anyone in the house stirred. In years past, long nights of drinking until the sun rose had been so frequent that it wasn't uncommon for them to go straight from boozing to PT sessions, having never even gone to sleep in between. Those days were long gone and Marcus paid the price for the reenactment of his glory days.

In his drunken stupor, he hadn't bothered to close the blinds before passing out. He was too concerned with falling asleep before the spins caused him to puke all over his bedroom. Now, his stupidity cost him, and he paid dearly. The light shining through the window directly into his face made his brain throb in his skull, threatening to ooze free from any hole available.

It was hot in his bedroom. Rhode Island was in the midst of a heatwave, and the breeze coming off of the pond only did so much. What could only be described as pure alcohol seeped from his pores, leaving the bed sheets beneath him drenched. The warm, damp sheet clung to Simpson's body as he rolled out of bed. He stood up slowly, but his stomach lurched and sent him to his knees. It took all of his willpower not to spread a fresh coating of stomach bile, chicken wings, and alcohol across the freshly polished hardwood floor.

Simpson stayed on his knees for what seemed like an eternity until the wave of nausea passed. The floor was vomit free, for now.

Grabbing his phone off the bedside table, Simpson groaned when he realized it was almost 2 P.M.

We really poured it on last night. I wonder how everyone else is managing.

Simpson opened the messaging app on his phone, pulled up the group text thread, and tapped away at the screen. He stopped when he realized he had no reception.

"You've got to be fucking kidding me."

Simpson tossed the phone on the bed before making his way across the room to his suitcases. He remembered the warmth of the sweat on his sheets and suddenly wasn't so sure that it had been sweat. He wasn't about to smell the sheets to find out, but he was thankful he had stripped nude before passing out and hadn't pissed his pants as well.

Not bothering to put undergarments on—it was hot as hell and Simpson hated the feeling of sweaty balls—he pulled his sweatpants over his ass, popping a semi chub as the soft material rubbed across the head of his cock. He adjusted his crotch, tucking his cock into his waistband so as not to draw attention to his half erect hang down. Simpson grabbed a tank top with an old DMX album printed on the chest and threw it over his head. It had been years since X put out a good album, but Simpson couldn't let the tank top go. He'd had the thing for over a decade, and although the threadbare top was ready for the garbage, Simpson wasn't ready to put it there.

Dressed and still a bit drunk, Simpson exited the bedroom, not quite ready to grab the day by the balls, but after some breakfast and a Monster energy drink, he soon would be.

* * *

In various states of inebriation, the guys gather around the kitchen. Simpson was eating a peanut butter and jelly sandwich with Doritos smashed in between the two slices of bread. Everyone looked at him with disgust, especially after last night's escapades, but Simpson considered the concoction a delicacy. The crunch made the sandwich. It didn't have to be Doritos, any chip would do, but Simpson preferred the cheesy tortilla chips above all else.

The aroma of scrambled eggs, bacon, and French toast permeated every inch of the kitchen, and anyone not too hungover to eat waited with bated breath for breakfast to finish. Haney, Finger, and Paul were laboring in the kitchen. Everyone else was still too fucked up to help.

Simpson watched as Haney grabbed plates from the cabinet and set them at the large dining room table. Paul went around the room and loaded everyone's plates up with breakfast. "Dig in," he said.

They didn't have to be told twice. All of them were used to shoveling food into their mouths at the cyclic rate, never stopping to enjoy what they were eating. Sure, it tasted good, but food was fuel, and even after all these years most of the guys still had trouble sitting down and tasting their food rather than inhaling it.

Simpson scarfed down his meal, sitting in silence and watching his brothers eat, waiting for them to finish so he could get the ball rolling.

Micha was the last one finished, and although Simpson

himself was still feeling the alcohol, Micha's struggle to hold in the foul contents of his stomach was amusing.

"Alright guys, last night was a hell of a time, but you all know as well as I do that I didn't arrange for you fuckwads to come out here and get shitfaced." Simpson walked across the dining room, continuing his speech. "Frankly, I'm surprised Paul made it the entire night without trying to fight one of us. I guess you have changed since Waikiki, right, Paul?"

"I'll have you know I haven't gotten into a single bar fight in like five years," Paul said.

Everyone laughed and Simpson continued on.

"That's good, Paul. Glad to see you don't beat the shit out of people for fun anymore," Simpson said, smiling. "I don't either, and sometimes, I miss that part of me, but that crazy son of a bitch had to go. But in all seriousness, we need to go about this weekend as distraction free as possible. So, if you will all kindly drop your cell phones into the bag when I bring it around I would appreciate it."

"Fuck you," Simpson heard someone yell, causing everyone to laugh.

"Simpson, I told you I need my phone and my laptop," Haney said.

"Yeah, Haney, you're the exception. I don't understand one bit about what the fuck you're doing, or why the fuck someone would *pay* to watch you play video games, but if it's your livelihood, I'll get you the Wi-Fi info and you can keep your phone." Simpson stretched, walking over to the sink where he retrieved a garbage bag from the cabinet underneath it. "The rest of you though? You pricks aren't getting the Wi-Fi, and I know there is no reception out here, so just put the damn phones in. You can all have them back at night. I just want to make sure we actually try to go hard on the healing process."

Simpson went around collecting the phones, everyone eventually tossing their sacred devices into the bag, even if for some of them it was akin to removing one of their balls. The phones were nothing more than another form of addiction, and while Simpson knew it was unrealistic to keep them indefinitely, he intended on minimizing everyone's time behind a screen.

He'd only allowed Haney the exception because it was the only way to get him to agree to make the trip. If the Devil Dog turned fucking nerd were to be believed, he made well into the six figures a year mark, and appeared to be on the road to becoming a millionaire. Simpson didn't understand the streaming games bullshit, but the way Haney explained it, having a schedule, and doing your best to adhere to it were key tenets of taking his profession to the next level. Simpson wanted that for Haney. He wanted success for all of them.

Simpson looked around the room, finally realizing that Ray was nowhere to be seen.

"Where's Hughes?" he asked.

When nobody responded, Simpson made his way to Ray's room. As much as they could all use the sleep, and Simpson knew Ray was the last one to bed, he felt like now was a good time to get the son of a bitch off his ass, get some food into the man, and get started with helping his friend cope with the trauma ruining his life before it was too late.

Simpson knocked on the door. "Put your prick away man, it's time to get up," Simpson said, busting Ray's balls. The door was slightly ajar, and as Simpson knocked, it opened further. He pushed the door open the rest of the way, entering the room. "I'm coming in," he said.

The room was empty.

"Shit," Simpson said.

A hand clapped Simpson on the shoulder. It was Finger.

"Relax, he probably went for a walk. It's a beautiful day outside. The guy has trouble sleeping, so maybe he decided to walk the alcohol off in peace."

Simpson nodded. "Yeah, maybe." But no matter what way you sliced it, Ray's absence didn't sit right with him. His gut felt heavy with dread. A sinking feeling, like everything was about to blow up in his face. Like when you just knew there was an IED in the road, and you knew you were going to run it over, but you didn't know when.

He hoped he was wrong, but he had learned to trust his instinct a long time ago. For now, there wasn't much they could do except wait, and if too much time had passed, go out and search for their missing friend.

He hoped they weren't too late to save Ray.

TWENTY
THE STREAM MUST GO ON

As everyone went off to check out the grounds and have some fun while reconnecting, Robert Haney spent the early afternoon setting up his streaming equipment. He felt like death, and looked about as good as he felt, but the stream must go on. He was a cunt hair away from taking his stream up a notch in sponsorships. If he could keep a consistent schedule and continue making engaging content, this time next year he very well might hit the seven-figure earnings mark.

The guys used to bust his balls back in Hawaii, tell him what a fucking nerd he was. They used to tell him he was going to die a virgin, because he preferred to spend weekends in the barracks playing Halo and Gears of War instead of hitting up the bars and chasing pussy. He didn't even under-stand where that bullshit came from; he hadn't been a virgin back then, but that didn't stop everyone from calling him one. The heckling had gotten so bad, that one time Haney *did* go out for a night drinking with the guys, and one of their buddies, Hinther, had paid a prostitute to fuck him.

Normally, Haney wouldn't have gone for shit like that. He

might have been a bit of a geek, but he didn't pay for pussy. Hinther knew that, so they kept it a secret from him, crafting an elaborate prank.

The guys thought it would be funny to have the hooker pose as a random woman out for drinks at the bar, spending the night flirting with him until he finally took her to a hotel. It wasn't difficult for the hooker to act normal. The prostitutes of Waikiki were not the strung out, haggard looking whores of other states. Of course, *some* of them looked that way, but in Waikiki, many of them ranged from average looking women, to absolute smoke show.

Haney didn't know for sure, but he supposed it had something to do with the cost of living in Hawaii. He guessed it probably happened more often than one would think, considering it's not something that's likely to cross the mind unprovoked. But he assumed these women moved to the island for college, only to find that they couldn't afford to actually live in Hawaii. Rather than flip burgers, they sold pussy. They must have made a fortune looking the way they did.

The guys never told him how much they paid her, but it had to have been a considerable amount, because she spent hours at the bar with them knocking drinks back. When it was all said and done, it had been weeks before someone finally spilled the beans, and even then Hinther had only come clean because when they were all out on a training operation a few weeks later, Haney's dick started burning when he took a piss and Hinther had to convince him to go get his bore punched by medical. The hooker was selling her pussy as part of a bundle, every fuck comes free with the clap.

Still, he couldn't place the blame squarely on those assholes; it had been his choice to bareback a stranger.

Nerd or not, what was more important was the fact that Haney was now a success story, and it sounded foolish to call the man a nerd for playing games for hundreds of thousands of dollars a year.

Having finished setting up the last piece of equipment, a green screen, Haney powered on his laptop. The laptop itself was overkill, much stronger than need be for streaming. The damn thing blew most people's home PC away. Haney could easily afford the overpriced piece of hardware, but lucky for him, his platform had grown large enough that there wasn't a PC gaming company in the free market that *wouldn't* toss a sponsorship his way. The gaming world was at his fingertips, and he wouldn't have it any other way.

After a few minutes of running through preliminary tests, making sure everything was working properly, Haney sent a tweet out to his followers notifying them the stream would go live in five minutes. The trip had only thrown off his schedule by a few hours, but he had been sure to tell all of his followers to monitor social media, as he would stream from a new location and the schedule would adjust accordingly. He hoped the time difference wouldn't negatively affect his donations, but if they did, it's not like he was strapped for cash.

Haney grabbed a t-shirt from one of his sponsors—an energy drink company that targeted gamers—threw the shirt over his head and grabbed the container of energy powder. It wasn't required, but Haney liked to start the stream off with product placement. The residual income from viewers using his coupon code for various sponsors added up to a nice chunk of change.

No time like the present, Haney thought. He cracked his knuckles, cleared his throat, and clicked the stream button.

Time to make that money.

* * *

B illy's phone pinged. He reached into his pocket, pulling out his smartphone. The notification lit up his screen, illuminating the otherwise dark bedroom. He read the message, tapping the notification and smiling as he did so. His favorite streamer, *Insaney Haney* was live. Billy never missed any of Haney's streams, and was disappointed when he read online that Haney was on a vacation and it may interrupt his normal screening schedule. He wished Haney had kept the schedule, but a few hours late was better than nothing at all.

Billy thought *Insaney Haney* was one of the good ones, a genuine dude. He seemed nice, and while he played to current trends, he also dedicated certain days of the week to playing the things he was passionate about. Billy was happy to pay the monthly subscription fee for the hours of entertainment Haney provided. Hell, he figured the 4.99 a month was a steal, and was known to drop a few hundred a month in additional donations. Haney kept a ticker that tracked donations, and Billy was proud to be the top donor every month.

He rolled off of his bed and jumped into his massive gaming chair, a piece of equipment he was incredibly proud of. It had cost him half a grand and even had a built-in cooler that could hold up to six cans of soda. Hell, the only thing it couldn't do was suck him off. Luckily, his pocket pussy handled that task with ease. Speaking of Jenna, he made a reminder on his phone to wash that fine piece of rubber snatch, he couldn't remember the last time he had cleaned it.

Billy clicked away at the computer, loading Haney's stream on one monitor, and his PlayStation on the other. Adept at multitasking, he intended on powering through Persona 5 while also watching Haney do what he does best. Sure, it might be a bit ridiculous for him to be playing a game and watching someone else play at the same time, but Billy felt like he didn't have another choice in the matter. He was as addicted to playing video games as he was to watching Haney play video games. Asking him to choose between playing his favorite game or watching his favorite streamer was like asking him to choose which one of his parents he wanted to kill. He'd choose both of them.

The game booted up as Haney's stream started.

Haney's voice came through Billy's top of the line speakers, crystal clear. "What's up, guys? Insaney Haney here, live from a cabin in the middle of nowhere. Apologies for the late stream, but this trip came up last minute, and a few of my old Marine Corps buddies have been really struggling lately. I know you guys like me to be predictable, and I'm really sorry, but I'm thankful for those of you who are able to watch the delayed stream. If the quality is a bit low, I apologize, but I think we can still have a good time."

While navigating the Phantom Thieves through the labyrinthine mind of an unfortunate soul in need of a change of heart, Billy saw the splash screen for Friday the 13th: The Game pop up on his second monitor. Haney's face was in the bottom left corner of the screen.

Ok, Friday the 13th, I can fuck with that, Billy thought. The game was buggy as hell, but watching Jason maim, disembowel, and dismember the counselors was incredibly satisfying. And as a fan of the series, the attention to detail in the settings, and Kane Hodder motion captured kill sequences definitely gave the game some sorely needed bonus points. Hell, even the bugs could be fun sometimes. Billy might pay closer attention to the stream than he had expected.

He rocked back and forth in his chair, furiously tapping his leg. Drinking upwards of three cans of energy drinks a day, Billy frequently had to piss like a racehorse. He paused his game and flew to the bathroom.

Once finished draining the lizard, Billy plopped back into his chair, the shocks easily absorbing the strain placed on them.

Unpausing his game, Billy decided he would give this dungeons boss one more try, and win or lose, devote his full attention to Haney's stream.

After having his ass thoroughly handed to him, Billy tossed the controller on his bed and turned his gaze to the stream.

The image quality suffered because of Haney's change of location, that was for sure.

Man, the Wi-Fi at that cabin must suck, Billy thought, scratching his balls. He flicked away a bit of ball cheese that had gotten stuck on his fingernail.

The gameplay was choppy, even for Friday the 13th standards, and Haney's webcam feed was grainy and scrambled. Billy appreciated the effort to give his fans a stream, even from a remote location, but the quality was bad enough he was considering donating a few bucks to Haney and going back to Persona—if he didn't beat this boss tonight, he was going to lose his fucking mind.

Billy picked up a giant drum of store brand cheese balls, lifting it over his head and dumping them into his mouth. Believe it or not, cheese balls and Monster was a delicious combo, and nobody could tell Billy otherwise. He picked a loose ball off of his chair and plopped it into his mouth.

With great reluctance, Billy was about to exit his web browser when he noticed something odd in the corner of Haney's stream. It was tough to tell through all the visual distortion, but it looked as if a large man was standing in the corner of whatever room Haney was in.

Details were scarce because of the low-resolution image —all Billy could tell for sure was the man had a chest length beard and arms that would make The Rock jealous.

Something about it didn't sit right with Billy. Haney would never have someone standing in the background of his stream, even in a new location. Billy knew Haney would not be so careless, so unprofessional.

He leaned forward in his chair, trying to get a better look at the stream.

The man moved forward, the video buffering causing frames to skip, making it appear as if he teleported behind Haney. He grabbed Haney by the back of the head and smashed his skull into his setup. The camera fell over, leaving the image turned on its side.

Billy couldn't see what was happening anymore, but what he heard he didn't like.

* * *

Hughes entered the back door of the cabin. She was everywhere now. In the house, in the woods, even in his friends.

After he had fled the cabin, he hid in the woods, wanting to be left alone. But as his friends left the cabin to go about their "healing," he noticed something strange. The dead woman had taken them the same way she had taken him. The change was subtle, and at first he hadn't seen it. But if he looked close enough, he could see flashes of her within them, like an out-of-place frame spliced into a piece of film.

She was there, and then she wasn't.

He was losing his mind, or he wasn't.

Ray wasn't about to stick around and find out. He needed to get the fuck out of there, and fast.

143

The cabin door swung shut behind him and Ray was back overseas. Sand whipped by him, stinging his eyes. A brownout, of course. The sand storm was so thick he couldn't see his dick to take a piss if he were to whip it out right now. But how did he get here?

Gunfire filled the air and Ray ducked, searching for cover and concealment, but finding none. He ran, the sand parting like the Red Sea, allowing him to see in front of him. He felt lighter than he should have, and realized he wasn't wearing equipment, just jeans and a T-shirt. He had no weapons to speak of. No rifle, no side arm. Why would he leave the wire without his gear?

He heard the dying screams of men and women, explosions in the distance.

His mind was playing tricks on him: one moment he was in the cabin, the next he was in the desert.

He continued along the path of torment. Broken and crippled bodies, mangled and maimed, lay strewn about the path, leading him toward some unknown end.

His heart pumped with blood, adrenaline flowing through him. The large vein in his temple pounding against the skin, threatening to burst from its thin, fleshy prison.

An explosion behind him sent him flying forward, face hitting the sand, scraping it. Pushing himself off the ground, blood seeped from abrasions on his cheek, hitting the ground below him.

But the ground below him was made of carpet, not the brown dirt he had been walking on a few moments ago. Hughes looked around, getting his bearings straight.

He was back in the cabin.

A moment later, the desert again.

Ray didn't know where he was anymore, couldn't separate the flashback from reality. Trapped in a dream so vivid it might as well be real. Maybe it was? He could not think straight, and was unable to separate the construct of his mind from the fabric of the tangible, real world.

He turned around again, standing in front of a closed door.

Ray opened the door and walked into the bedroom, standing behind Haney.

The Marine infantryman's primary mission was to locate, close with, and destroy the enemy. Trapped in his flashback, Hughes could no longer differentiate between friend or foe.

* * *

Haney heard the loud footsteps behind him but before he turned around, a large hand gripped him by the back of his head and smashed his face into the laptop. The tough, metal casing cracked, but the laptop didn't break. The webcam tumbled from its mount on top of the computer.

In an instant, Haney's fight-or-flight instinct kicked in. He tried to turn and throw a punch, but his assailant caught his fist, turned it inward, and wrenched down.

The force of the downward pressure cracked his wrist, and an intense burning sensation radiated through his arm.

Haney's entire upper body followed his arm, and as he was falling flat on his face, his attacker brought his knee up, meeting Haney's jaw halfway. Shooting stars exploded across his vision. The strike slammed his teeth together, sending shattered pieces of teeth sprinkling to the floor and down his throat. Blood poured from his mouth, and when Haney tried to speak, his voice was too garbled to understand.

The vicious strike sent him flat on his back. He tried to roll over to his knees and regain his footing, but his attacker struck out with his foot, smashing his heel into the side of Haney's face.

Haney crashed to the ground with such an impact that his body bounced off the floor before coming to rest. He tried to sit up and scoot backwards, giving himself some space, time to recuperate.

Running out of room, Haney kicked his chair, sending it flying into the knees of the man. The impact was weak and did nothing more than piss him off. His attacker leaned forward and threw the chair aside. The brief pause in the beating that was bestowed upon Haney allowed him to see his attacker eye to eye for the first time.

It was Ray.

"What the fuck?" Haney said. He didn't know why Ray was beating his ass, but his old squad mate looked ready to move in for the kill.

Haney stood up, woozy but not ready to give up. With Ray closing in quickly, Haney waited a moment for him to get closer before launching a kick at his midsection.

Ray's forward momentum lent the blow a greater impact, but even with the added force pain didn't seem to register on his face.

Haney threw a punch, but it was slow and weak. Ray dodged it and rammed his forehead into Haney's nose. It shattered, an explosion of blood coating both men. Ray grabbed Haney's body as he was collapsing and lifted him off of his feet. He carried him like a rag-doll, Haney's attempts at self-defense now weak and useless.

Stopping at the window, Ray let Haney fall to the ground.

Haney, flat on his back, lifted his arms, trying to defend himself but the vicious punches that Ray slammed down upon him were too quick, too strong. Unable to deflect the punishing blows, Haney's face transformed into a battered and broken mess. His eyes swelled up, almost completely closed. He was a lumpy, unidentifiable mess.

Ray lifted Haney off the floor and smashed his face through the window.

Haney screamed in agony as broken shards of glass tore at his skin, ripping and tearing the flesh. A jagged piece of glass pierced through his swollen eyelid, impaling the orb behind it. Gelatinous ocular fluid oozed from the ruined eyeball, dripping down Haney's cheek.

Ray loosened his grip on Haney, letting him collapse to the floor where he writhed in pain. His gasps came short and labored. He felt a rattling in his chest as he coughed up blood.

"Why?" Haney croaked, coughing up more blood.

Not saying a word, Ray grabbed a six-inch shard of glass from the window and jabbed it into Haney's throat, ripping it from one side to the other, painting his own face with bright red arterial spray.

Haney's last moments streamed live over the internet as thousands of viewers listened to the carnage, only catching snippets of video from the displaced camera, trying to determine if what they were hearing was real, or some elaborate online prank.

TWENTY-ONE
COCAINE'S A HELL OF A DRUG

Micha and Mark sat at a picnic table overlooking the lake. The view was immaculate, and if it weren't for the heat, it would be the perfect place to get fucked up. Neither of the two wanted anyone else to know what they were doing. They didn't think Saint Marcus Simpson would approve, so they had to strike out on their own for some privacy.

Simpson and Paul had invited them to do some axe throwing, and while that sounded fucking badass to Micha, he thought it would be more badass to do it after he and Mark did a few bumps.

Micha didn't give a shit that Simpson turned straight edge after almost offing himself, and frankly he wasn't here because he needed help. Not that he didn't agree that he had drug problems. No, he was well aware of that. Micha simply couldn't care less. He was here for the prospect of partying, reliving his glory days. He hadn't realized Simpson had turned into Captain Bumout, otherwise he'd have stayed in Hawaii, doing Ice and smashing strippers.

Simpson could try to take the wind out of their sails all he wanted, but in the end the years of partying, hard living, and the atrocities they witnessed meant that no matter how good they were doing, there was a little demon trapped within all of them, always there, waiting for a slipup. Rather than live his life in some sort of constant war with himself, Micha embraced his demons . That demon likes to get fucked up and blow shit up. Blowing shit up with mortars wasn't exactly legal for U.S. citizens, so that really only left them with one option as far as Micha was concerned.

Lucky for him, Mark felt the same way. The two of them didn't see eye to eye much while they served together, but had reconnected after their contracts ended, even getting a place together and partying it up like their lives depended on it.

Maybe their lives did depend on it. What did the two of them have to live for if you took away the fun of getting fucked up? Neither of them had any friends or relatives, that were part of the reason they'd both enlisted to begin with. And making *new* friends? That had been proven to require nothing less than a miracle after everything they'd been through. Some people just couldn't readjust to civilian life, at least Micha and Mark had the balls to admit it to themselves that they were amongst that group.

"I can't believe you scored," Micha said.

Mark chopped the coke up with his driver license. "Yeah, well, it was just dumb luck. I went to take a leak last night and a few guys were banging lines off the sink. I did a bump with them, and by the end of the night I had gotten one of them to serve me. Actually, I think I got this from the same guy that sold the weed to Haney."

"Thank God, man, because I really wouldn't be able to stand all this sissy shit Simpson is up to out here. He really thinks he can save us, like he's a fucking pastor or something.

I don't need to be saved, I need to get high, and I need to get my dick sucked."

"I hear you on that. I don't care what he says. Maybe I have a problem. Actually, I do, but the difference is I *know* I do. I don't care. I'm living my life how I want. I looked death in the face already. I've made peace with the fact I can go at any time and I've decided that I'm going to do whatever the fuck I want with however much time I have left. Ray though? Now *that* is a guy that need's Simpson's bullshit. He's a basket case, you can tell just looking at him. He's tapped in the fucking head."

"You're right about that. He's certifiable. I'm surprised the judge let him out on bail. He owes Simpson a blowie for that, because one look at the man will tell you he shouldn't be allowed in public."

"Fuck it, I feel bad for the guy, but c'mon. We were all there. He needs to stop being such a cunt about it," Mark said.

Leaning forward, he used an index finger to press one nostril closed, running his face across a line of coke, snorting the wonderful powder.

Micha watched, a slight tremor going through his body as he waited his turn for a bump.

"God damn," Mark laughed, sliding the mirror to Micha, who wasted no time burying his face in the white powder.

Looking up from the coke, Micha was feeling it already. The coke was top-notch. "Did you get that guy's number? This is some good shit," he said.

Mark didn't respond. His lips were a shade of blue and he seemed to look *through* Micha, rather than at him.

"Yo, man, are you good?" Micha asked.

Mark's body tensed as foam frothed at the corners of his mouth. He shook, almost imperceptibly at first, but soon the intensity ratcheted up, and Micha knew his friend was overdosing.

Micha jumped up from the picnic table and ran to Mark. He grabbed him by the shoulders, lowering him to the ground and placing him on his side. He wasn't sure if that was the right thing to do in this situation; he thought maybe it was in case of vomiting, but Micha thought vomiting was the last of Mark's worries at the moment.

"I'm going to get you some help," he said, running toward the house. He needed to get an ambulance here as soon as possible.

An immense pain tore through Micha's knee and right ass cheek, followed by the sound of two quick shots. The bullets traveled at such a speed that they had taken him out just as he heard the shots. It was an AR-15, a sound which Micha was well acquainted.

Blood poured from his ruined knee, and his ass felt as if it were on fire. Micha tried to get up, but his knee couldn't support the full weight of his body and he collapsed.

An explosion of dirt burst from the ground a few feet in front of his face. Micha looked in the direction the gunshot had come from.

Hughes stomped out of the tree line, rifle in hand, hanging at his side. He closed the distance between them with a speed Micha would have thought impossible for a man Ray's size, but before he could make sense of what he was seeing, Ray was dragging him by the collar, back toward the picnic tables.

"What the fuck, man, what are you doing? Mark needs help," Micha pleaded, knowing that Ray shot him, but still trying to appeal to him, as if he hadn't just been shot by the man whose mental state had deteriorated beyond repair, and was now dragging his wounded ass across the dirt.

Stopping at the picnic table opposite where Mark lay in the dirt. Ray lifted Micha off the ground and smashed his face against the table.

Once. Twice. Three times. A loud crack accompanied the third impact, and blood leaked out of Micha's ear, leaving a crimson trail down his neck.

He jammed the rifle's buttstock against the back of Micha's head, squishing his face against the table.

Twice, Ray lifted the rifle and cracked the back of Micha's head with the butt. He lifted it overhead, poised to deliver a third and final crushing blow to Micha's skull, but stopped as suddenly as he had started the attack.

Ray threw the rifle down and wrapped his arm around Micha's neck, using his free arm to push down on the back of his head.

He had Micha in a rear naked choke. Micha struggled to rip Ray's arm off of his throat, but he was too dazed from the blows to the head to muster a competent defense against the hold.

Keeping the blood choke tight, Ray continued to apply pressure to the back of Michas's head while lowering his face to the cocaine on the picnic table.

He held Micha's face in the powder, applying more pressure to the hold. He applied pressure to Micha's windpipe rather than the carotid artery, transitioning from a blood choke to cutting off Micha's airway.

Micha tried to hold his breath. He wasn't sure how much longer he could hold out. He desperately needed to breathe, but he was face first in a mountain of coke, and although he had done a nice rail, watching Mark OD on the stuff had him feeling like it was laced with something crazy, like fentanyl. Mark was a heavy user, and one bump shouldn't have done him in.

No, Micha had no intention of snorting any more of this shit, but he couldn't help it. Blackness crept across the outer edges of his vision until everything was blurry.

He gasped for air, the action an involuntary response just as Ray let go of the choke, sending an immense mountain of cocaine straight up his nostrils.

Micha coughed and gagged while Ray brought his face in for another hit of the coke.

The drugs flooding his senses dulled the pain, and Micha felt disoriented. Although his body had been starved for oxygen before, the fentanyl lacing the coke slowed his breathing further, even after Ray allowed Micha an open airway.

As hypoxia set in, Ray let Micha's body crumple to the ground next to the discarded AR-15.

He crossed the table where Mark lay motionless on the ground. He stood over Mark for a moment before kicking the body. There was no movement, no sign whether or not he was alive. If there was a rise and fall of the chest, the breaths were too shallow to notice.

Bending over, he removed Mark's prosthetic leg, raised it over his head and swung it down, smashing Mark's cheekbone.

He brought it down again, and again, rearranging Mark's face. Shattered teeth spilled from his mangled face. Another blow to the cheek popped Mark's eye out of the socket. The optic nerve remained attached to the eye, leaving it dancing against his cheek.

Ray continued assaulting Mark's corpse with the prosthetic until it broke, becoming difficult to grasp for a good swing.

Ray removed the metal limb from the broken socket piece, tossing the joint housing aside.

With the metal portion of the limb in hand, Ray stomped on Mark's head. The bones in his cranium shattered, and Ray stomped once more for good luck. Flakes of skull burst forth, flying about, and brain matter squirted out from the opening in Mark's head. A chunky soup of skull fragments, blood, and crushed brain matter pooled around his wrecked head.

Ray ceased the attack, staring down at Mark's mangled corpse. The desecrated, grisly remains showed no indication of overdose, only the gruesome remains of a brutalized body.

Ray turned around and walked back to Micha, who was either dead or dying.

With a grunt, Ray rammed the metal prosthetic into Micha's mouth. It punched through the back of his throat and stuck in the ground beneath Micha. His body quivered a bit, feet trembling before the body was still.

Ray got down on one knee and patted down the body. Inside Micha's boot, he found a KA-BAR sheathed in an ankle holder. He removed the knife from its sheath and tucked it between his belt and waistband.

The brutal assault over, he picked up the rifle and stalked off into the woods from which he appeared, leaving the bodies of his former squad mates to fester in the sun.

TWENTY-TWO
THROWING AXE

T he sun reflected off of the axe, sending beams of light scattering about as it flipped through the air. The flat end struck the target low, sending the throwing axe tumbling to the ground.

Finger laughed. "Nice try, but it's not as easy as you thought, is it?"

"No," Simpson said, picking up another axe. "It's not."

Simpson looked around, taking in the beauty of the woods surrounding the target area. "I can't believe I got them to fund this trip. We're really lucky to have this opportunity."

He raised his arms over his head, gripping the axe. He stepped forward and launched the deadly instrument; it flipped end over end, this time completely missing the target. Another lame duck throw. Clearly throwing bladed weapons wasn't Simpson's strong suit.

"Damn, I showed up just in time for the show," Paul said, coming out of the tree line.

"Where the hell did you come from, you fucking creep?" Simpson said.

"I was checking out the hiking trails. There are so many

good ones. I could spend all weekend just exploring this place," Paul said.

Simpson nodded. "Yeah, this property really is something special. Go for it, if that's what you want to do. I'll check out some trails with you later on. I'm sure some of the other guys would love to check them out, too."

Two loud cracks echoed through the trees.

"What the fuck was that?" Finger asked.

"Sounded like a rifle," said Paul

"Yeah, it did. But it wasn't coming from the range," Simpson pointed behind them. "The range is that way."

"You think it's that hillbilly, Micha, just fucking around?" Finger asked.

"I hope so," Simpson said.

Finger sucked his teeth. "But you don't think so?"

"If you're asking me that, you don't either. Jesus, if one of them just swallowed a bullet, I'm not going to be able to live with that."

"Simpson, if one of them swallowed a bullet, there wouldn't have been two shots," said Paul.

"Fuck, you're right." Simpson tossed the keys to the van at Finger. "Take those keys, you get to the van and wait. If you don't hear from anyone in fifteen minutes, get out of here and get the police. If you hear anything fucked up, same thing. Don't play hero, get the fuck out of dodge and get help."

"You don't think…"

Simpson cut him off. "I don't know what I think."

Finger looked at Paul. "You wait here, just in case he comes back."

"I'm not waiting here, Finger."

"Just fucking stay here. Please. Haney should be finished with his stream any time now, and we don't need him walking around the woods by himself. He's a fucking gaming nerd, do you think he's going to be able to find his way around here? Give it fifteen minutes. If you don't hear from anyone, then you can do what you gotta do. We don't even know for sure if anything is wrong."

The three men went their separate ways, Simpson running toward the gunfire, Finger navigating the winding dirt trail back to the cabin, and Paul awaiting *something* to happen.

Simpson didn't know what was going on, and as much as he hoped it was only Micha fucking around, that bad feeling in his stomach had gotten much worse.

TWENTY-THREE
A MACABRE MEMORIAL

P aul sat on a tree stump, whacking a throwing axe on the ground. It had only taken a few minutes of sitting on the sideline for boredom to set in, and although he had heckled Simpson about his axe throwing abilities, he gave the weapons a toss himself and quickly realized that axe throwing took skill. He gave up, and instead smacked the ground aimlessly, like a bored child waiting to be told he can come out of timeout.

He loved the woods here and was happy he had made the trip. The warm air and scent of fresh pine did almost as much to clear his mind as going toe to toe in the ring did for him. As a bonus, he didn't have to worry about concussions or life-threatening blows to the head when he was enjoying nature—he couldn't say that about boxing. Sometimes it took weeks for his head to feel right after a good sparring session. Partly because he had a habit of turning sparring matches into gym wars, and partly because when you've been blown up in a truck by IEDs as often as Paul had been, your brain is scrambled by default. It doesn't take much to rattle what's left in the attic.

Standing up and brushing the dirt of his shorts, Paul took action. As much as he enjoyed the scenery, something was up, and both Simpson and Finger could eat shit, as far as he was concerned. They weren't in charge out here—this wasn't the Marine Corps—and even if it was, you sure as shit didn't leave a man behind. Something was wrong, and Paul was going to take the initiative and do something about it, not sit on the bench and hope everything turned out fine.

Paul stepped off in the gunfire's direction, deciding to go through the woods rather than take the trail.

Ray emerged from the woods ahead of him, carrying an AR-15 by his side. He was coated in blood and gore. Pulpy globs of crimson and bone flakes littered his beard, his face a mask of blood. His shirt was covered with the same carnage.

As Ray exited the tree line, he dropped the AR-15 in the dirt without breaking stride.

"Jesus Christ dude, are you ok?" Paul asked.

Ray didn't respond.

Paul was about to ask again, thinking maybe Ray hadn't heard him. Tinnitus and hearing loss was a common thread among all of them, but as Ray got closer, Paul knew the truth.

"Listen, man, whatever is going on, we can figure it out," Paul said, hands up, backing away. A strange feeling tickled the back of Paul's neck, and his heart rate increased. His stomach was in knots. The same feeling he got overseas when shit was about to kick off. It was a sixth sense, and most men who've seen combat claim to develop something like it. Paul was experiencing it now, the first time he'd ever felt such a way stateside.

Ray closed the gap and Paul stopped backing up, digging his feet in and taking a fighting stance. He didn't want to fight Ray; the man was a behemoth, a specimen. He was as large as Simpson, and although Ray hadn't been known as a fighter back in Hawaii, the man was clearly unhinged and someone his size was going to be a problem, no matter how good Paul was in the ring.

"Come any closer and I'm going to fuck you up," Paul warned, not fully believing his own posturing.

Ray stepped in, throwing a haymaker with enough force to flatten anyone standing in front of it.

Paul quickly took a step forward, throwing a jab at Ray's face as he did so. The blow landed cleanly, snapping Ray's head back. The movement combined with the quick punch was enough to throw Ray's haymaker wide off target, and Paul used the opportunity to fire off a one, two, three combo —a jab, straight right, left hook to the body.

The punches all landed cleanly, the straight right snapping Ray's nose, sending blood spraying forth from the now crooked piece of cartilage. The hook to the body landed perfectly, but Ray was solid, and despite the force and perfect placement, it did little to stop him.

"I don't want to hurt you, Ray, but I swear to God I'll break your fucking face," Paul said.

Ray advanced again, walking into two more punches. The punches snapped his head back, but he ate them like they were breakfast, closing the distance between the two men, smothering Paul's ability to put mustard on the punches.

Ray wrapped his arms around Paul, bear hugging him. He squeezed, the muscles and tendons in his arms, back, and neck rippled from the strain.

Paul gritted his teeth and tried to break the hold, but it was no use. Ray was strong as an ox.

Ray head-butted Paul, but Paul turned his head at the last minute, saving his nose and taking the hit on the cheek instead. It hurt like a son of a bitch, but a bruised cheek was a better outcome than a shattered nose.

Ray squeezed harder, and Paul swore he heard something pop. He thought his ribs might break if he couldn't get Ray to loosen his grip. In a last ditch effort, he used the one technique that negates a man's physicality.

He thrust his knee forward as hard as he could, ramming it into Ray's cock and balls.

The effect was instant. Ray dropped Paul in the dirt and fell to the ground, cupping his battered ballsack.

Both men writhed in pain. Paul stood, knowing this might be his only chance. He didn't want anyone else to get hurt. Maybe if he could restrain Ray, nobody else would suffer.

Paul removed his belt from the loops of his cargo shorts. He ran the long end through the belt, twisting it and bringing it back, turning the belt into makeshift handcuffs.

The effects of the nut shot were subsiding, Ray was already rising to his feet.

Paul jumped on his back, ramming his knee into Ray's spine and pressing down. He tried to use the force of the blow to drive Ray into the ground, but Ray flipped over and reached into his boot, pulling a shiny object from it.

It took Paul a moment to realize what the object was, and before Paul could react, Ray drove the KA-BAR into his gut, twisting and wriggling the knife around.

Ray grabbed the handle with his free hand and, using a two handed grip, pulled hard to the left, tearing the flesh and exposing the delicate organs within. Blood gushed out, and he grabbed the intestines and pulled, removing foot after foot of the digestive system.

With Paul's feces factory lying in the dirt beside him, Ray took the KA-BAR and rammed it into Paul's chest. He yanked it out, and rammed it home again and again and again. Blood sprayed forth with each stab, in and out, in and out until the stab wounds were so close together it looked like one gaping, gore-drenched hole.

Ray removed the knife from Paul's mutilated corpse, staring at the dozens of stab wounds and eviscerated midsection before taking the KA-BAR and shoving it into Paul's neck. He ran the knife back and forth, cutting through flesh, tendon, and muscle. The knife stopped when it hit the spine, and Ray stepped on the corpse's shoulder for leverage. He worked the knife back and forth, putting his weight on the corpse while pulling its hair until at last the head came off with a sickening tearing noise.

Ray stripped Paul's boots from his feet, carrying the boots in one hand, and Paul's severed head in the other as he walked back to where he discarded the rifle. The blood dripping from the ragged stump of Paul's recently detached brain housing group left a trail in his wake, leading from the ax throwing pit to the tree line.

Ray set the hiking boots and head on the ground. Picking up the AR-15, he used the buttstock to scrape out a small divot in the ground. He balanced the rifle, buttstock first, barrel in the air, between the two boots. With the rifle now standing straight in the air, Ray mounted Paul's head atop the rifle.

With his grotesque sculpture complete, Ray retrieved a throwing axe from the pit and made his way back through the woods.

TWENTY-FOUR
CASUALTIES OF WAR

S impson bounded along the trail, choosing to stick to the path rather than risk injury running through the woods. The minutes felt like hours, and the more Simpson thought about the two rifle cracks, the more he didn't like the conclusions he drew.

His heart pounded in his chest, adrenaline coursed through his veins. He emerged from the trail in the woods, and his heart skipped a beat at the scene before him. Two bodies lie crumpled in the dirt at opposite ends of a picnic table.

Simpson ran to the table, not knowing what exactly he expected, but it sure as shit wasn't what he found.

He checked Mark's pulse and found nothing. Not that he expected a pulse. The broken prosthetic and battering of Mark's body told him all he needed to know. Foam had crusted along the corners of his mouth, and he knew that even if Mark hadn't been brutalized, there was a good chance he would still be dead. Simpson stood up and noticed the remnants of the cocaine on the picnic table.

Jesus Christ. How did I let this happen?

He rushed to the other side of the table and discovered another dead friend. The mangled face covered in blood and cocaine stopped him in his tracks. A bloody piece of prosthetic leg rose from Micha's mouth, like a flagpole had suddenly sprouted through his corpse. Simpson couldn't make sense of what he was seeing. He knew Ray needed help, and had violent outbursts, but this was something else entirely.

He sprinted to the cabin, and after a few minutes of running, had reached his destination. Entering through the back door, he crept along the hallways, stopping at doorways and entries into other areas. He had a small handgun in a safe in his room. Legally, he could carry the M&P Shield .40. He had a concealed carry permit but didn't feel comfortable hiding a loaded weapon wherever he went throughout his day.

Simpson entered his room, which looked exactly as he had left it. The house appeared to be empty, but Simpson knew he needed to act cautiously. Ray could be close by. He rummaged through his suitcase, removing the safe from it and retrieving his small, yet powerful handgun.

Not having heard a peep from within the cabin, Simpson did a quick search. He stopped in the dining room to grab his cell phone from the pillowcase he had put them all in. To his horror, the phones were scattered on the floor, smashed to bits. He rummaged through the pieces, hoping to find one that still worked, but they were all destroyed beyond use.

Not good, Simpson thought.

Stupid. I can't believe I was so stupid. I knew he was a danger to others; I had to try to make saving him my pet project, and now people are dead.

Simpson continued his search of the cabin, finding it

empty. He stopped in front of the only room he hadn't yet searched.

Haney's room.

He knocked on the door, not expecting a response. Deep down, he knew the carnage by the picnic tables was not the entirety of it.

As expected, silence greeted Simpson's knock. He kicked the door in, scanning the room like he was clearing a house overseas. The scene in Haney's room was grotesque.

Blood spatter stained the carpets and walls. Shards of broken glass from the shattered window littered the area. Across the room, slumped over in a computer chair was Haney. Simpson didn't have to see his face; he could tell by the tips of Haney's red mohawk. He crossed the room and turned the chair.

It was worse than he had imagined.

His arm was broken, bent at an impossible angle from the forearm. Shattered remnants of teeth filled his mouth, and the pieces that weren't left in his mouth were scattered along the floor. His jaw hung loose, and to the side of his face. Haney's cheeks were torn to ribbons, the meat below the flesh exposed and shredded.

His eyeball was missing.

Simpson threw up, spraying the vile, partially digested breakfast all over Haney's corpse, further desecrating his brother in arms.

When Simpson regained his composure, he had an idea.

Haney's computer. I can get through to 911 with it.

The modicum of hope the thought instilled within his heart evaporated the moment he looked at the laptop on the desk. The laptop was destroyed. Its screen shattered, the casing in pieces and the inside components smashed to bits. Haney's webcam had fallen off the top of the laptop onto the

169

table. In front of the camera, a ruined eyeball and the attached ocular nerve. A clear, jelly-like fluid oozed from the putrid peeper. Simpson didn't know if it landed there, or had been placed there. He wasn't sure he wanted to know.

Simpson puked again, this time expelling nothing more than a thin, yellowy substance.

The bile landed on the deflated orb, the foul smelling stomach contents mixing with the leaking ocular fluid, creating a ghoulish, soupy mixture.

Forcing himself to get a grip on the situation, Simpson knew that time was of the essence. The Warrior Retreat had turned into a lakeside massacre, and Simpson knew if he didn't get out of here with Finger and Paul, there would be more bloodshed.

Paul, he thought. *He's alone at the axe pit.*

Simpson kept the M&P Shield at the low-ready position; he needed to hurry, but be ready to fire at a moment's notice. The way things were going, the only way he was going to save lives was to take one himself.

TWENTY-FIVE
NO PRANK TODAY

Officer Wayne Bannon sat outside of Masters Homemade Donuts, enjoying a delicious, jelly-filled baked treat. He smacked his lips, and the powder fell on his uniform. It matched the jelly glob next to it nicely, in his opinion.

Not that Officer Bannon was a shit bag, donut eating fuck face of a cop—although he *was* a prick, to that he would concede—but he was intentionally trying to piss off his shift supervisor, Sergeant Dutch, who was notorious for being a fucking scumbag. He was just as likely to step on your dick for a promotion as he was to shoot first and ask questions later on a beat. Bannon had no time for pricks like him, and it gave him great pleasure to see the man seething in the patrol car directly next to his.

A crackle over the radio. "*All available units, we have a possible 0100 at the Lake Budlong Retreat property. Be advised, they described the suspect as a large man with a beard. We have no further information to go on.*"

Officer Bannon tossed the donut out the window, threw the vehicle into drive, and took off like a bat out of hell. He listened as the dispatcher continued relaying information. The call was an odd one.

The call came in from out of state, from one of those video game nerds. Said a man named "Insaney Haney" was playing Friday the 13th, and was murdered by a large man. 911 hung up and traced the call. It came from some guy named "Billy Gallo." The 911 dispatch wrote it off as one of those "swatting" pranks, where they claim someone is being held hostage to get a swat team sent out, but after tracing the IP, and doing some digging they discovered a recording of the incident. There was definitely an assault, but the feed went black. Assume the suspect is on site and dangerous.

Bannon steered the cruiser with one hand, rubbing his service pistol holster, thumbing its release with his shooting hand.

TWENTY-SIX
THERE ARE NO WINNERS IN WAR

Finger made it to the van, heavily winded and in a considerable amount of pain. Although he kept to the trail, in his haste he tripped on a tree root, falling face first into the dirt. He had some scrapes to show for it, none of them serious, but his ankle was fucked. He had felt something pop as he fell to the ground, and his ankle had blown up like a tick.

Like the world's biggest fucking moron, Finger had taken his shoe off to check the damage, only to realize it had swollen so much he couldn't put it back on. He didn't think it was broken, but it was a terrible sprain and it took entirely too long to get to the van.

The timeline Simpson had given him had long since passed, but Finger needed to give it more time. Marines didn't leave their own behind on the battlefield, and he would be damned if he was going to screw before he knew the shit had hit the fan. And if the shit hit the fan? Well, then at least he had the safety of the vehicle to protect him, and if need be, he could turn tail and haul ass out of there.

Finger opened the door and hopped into the driver's seat.

* * *

S impson made it back to the axe range far quicker than it had taken him to get from the range to the cabin. The brutality he found upon arrival was unlike anything he'd ever seen. Worse even than some of the war crimes he had seen some men commit all those years ago.

The macabre memorial was a sick play on the combat memorial he had seen so many times before. A mockery of the same monument his own friends had received overseas. Instead of a helmet sitting atop the rifle, Paul's decapitated head was the centerpiece of the memorial.

Simpson turned and ran toward the van. There would be time to mourn later. For now, Simpson had to hope Finger had gone for help.

* * *

E merging from the woods, Simpson was both happy to see Finger alive, seemingly unharmed, yet pissed that the man had not gone for help like he told him to.

"Finger, you were supposed to get help, you stubborn son of a bitch," Simpson said.

Finger got out of the van, holding onto the vehicle for support. He hobbled around, slowly making his way toward the passenger side. "I fucked my ankle up, man, you drive."

A loud grunt came from Simpson's left. He turned in time to see Ray launch the Hail Mary of all throwing axe tosses. Simpson watched in horror as the axed tumbled through the air before connecting with the back of Finger's skull, a wet crunching noise accompanying the impact.

Finger was knocked forward, falling face first onto the van. He slid down the exterior, crumpling in a heap.

Simpson couldn't believe his eyes. If it weren't for the axe being lodged in his friend's skull, he'd be jealous of the accuracy on display.

Simpson turned to Ray, taking a Weaver shooting stance. "Don't fucking move," he said.

Ray ignored the command and continued advancing toward Simpson. Simpson could see the vacancy in his eyes. Ray was no longer sitting in the driver's seat. Something had snapped inside of the man and there would be no reasoning.

Simpson couldn't pull the trigger. That part of him was buried. He wasn't a killer anymore. When he had arrived back stateside, he had no choice but to exile that part of him. Simpson didn't like to believe that the killer still lived inside of him, but he knew the truth. A part of him thirsted for blood. Killing a man does something to you, awakens something inside of the brain that cannot ever be cast aside completely. You could hide it, and hope that it stayed buried, but buried didn't mean dead. Taking another life would mean exhuming the part of him he had buried.

Simpson was afraid that if he killed Ray, he would enjoy it.

But there was another part of Simpson that had also been buried. The part of him that loved to beat the shit out of a man with his bare hands. The part of him that loved to fight. The Simpson that beat the brakes off of many a man who wrote a check with their mouth that their ass couldn't cash. It had been a long time since Marcus Simpson beat the shit out of someone, and he was excited to have another crack at it.

Putting the gun in the waistband of his pants, Simpson jogged toward Ray and as he got within an arm's distance, he swung for the fences.

The blow connected with a sickening *thwack*. Ray's orbital bone shattered. Blood oozed from the corner of his eye. The swelling and rearranged bone structure shut his eye instantly, but he didn't go down. Instead, he dropped his weight and did a double leg takedown on Simpson, driving him into the ground with the full force of his bodyweight.

An "oof" escaped Simpson as the air was driven out of him. He tried to scramble to his feet, but Ray was moving on autopilot and had already mounted Simpson.

Shit, Simpson thought. As Ray sat atop him, he remembered that his old friend had been an MMA fanatic. He wasn't sure how much training he had, but Simpson didn't want to find out.

A siren wailed in the distance, growing ever closer. It fell on deaf ears. Simpson heard nothing but the sound of his blood pumping through his veins.

Ray rained fists and elbows from above, and Simpson covered up, moving his upper body to dodge the blows. Ray got his licks in, but Simpson managed to use his arms and shoulders to negate the worst of it.

The intensity and frequency of the strikes diminished, and Simpson knew this was his chance, Ray was getting tired. Simpson threw his fist like a club, battering Ray's broken orbital bone.

"Fuck," Ray screamed as he fell off Simpson.

Simpson used the opportunity to stand up and go on the offensive. He was going to beat him within an inch of his life and personally drag his ass back to jail.

He stomped with all his weight, narrowly missing the target as Ray rolled in the dirt and rose to meet Simpson toe to toe once more.

Ray pulled the KA-BAR from a sheathe at his side, still wet blood painting the metal a nasty crimson.

Simpson saw the knife, and for the first time in years feared for his life.

He saw his life flash before his eyes.

Fishing on the pier with his older brother, Xavier.

Standing in front of Xavier's grave after he lost his life in Iraq, swearing to avenge him.

Sitting in the movie theater with his son, Anthony.

I've got to make it home, for Anthony.

The sirens drew closer, and behind Simpson a police cruiser slammed the brakes, skidding to a halt.

Simpson drew his gun, aiming it at Ray's chest. "Don't make me do it. If it's me or you, it ain't gonna be me, brother."

Ray hesitated.

"Ray, don't do this. You need help. You're going to go away for this, for a long time, but this isn't you man. Your mind isn't right. I saw your journal. I know what happened to you. I know what you saw. But your therapists are right man, there's no fucking ghost haunting you. Sleep paralysis is real, and I know you think what's happening to you is real, but it's not. It's in your head. I know it was years before those fucking morons at the VA told you about sleep paralysis, and you were convinced for so long that you were being haunted for what happened over there. But it wasn't your fault, man. It wasn't your fault."

Simpson thought he saw a glimmer of life in Ray's good eye and thought he might get through to him.

"Police, mother fucker, drop the gun or I swear to God I'll dump this entire magazine in your back," the cop yelled from behind Simpson.

Simpson ignored him. He had to have faith that the man was posturing, that he was trying to get Simpson to follow orders, but he knew the truth. If he didn't talk Ray down he was going to be leaving in a body bag.

"Ray, please. You need therapy. They have groups for this. They have medicine for this. I know you came off your meds. You hated the way they made you feel. But they have other meds, they can change the drug to something else. Trial and error until you find what works for you. It's too late to take back what you did. It's not too late to take responsibility for it and fix yourself."

Ray lowered the knife.

"Put the fucking gun down, last chance, asshole," the cop screamed.

A tear rolled down Ray's cheek. Simpson had gotten through to him.

Simpson extended his arms, welcoming Ray in for a hug.

Ray raised his arms too, accepting the hug. But as he got within arm's distance, he lunged at Simpson with the knife.

Simpson's firearm training kicked in, and he brought the gun up, firing three rounds straight into Ray's chest.

Ray crumpled to the ground.

Simpson heard five rounds fired, but only three were from his gun. Two rounds punched through his back, fired from Officer Bannon's service pistol.

He dropped the gun and clasped his chest.

As he removed his hand from his chest, he noticed blood coating his palm. One bullet had gone in through his back and exited his chest. The cops' aim had been perfect.

Simpson spat out blood, took two steps forward and collapsed next to Ray.

He struggled to breathe and the wet, rattling sounds coming from his chest drowned out whatever it was the cop was screaming at him.

The cop ran to where the two men lay in the dirt and holstered his weapon.

Officer Bannon keyed his radio and called for help as Simpson bled out. His vacant eyes stared into those of his dead squad mate, unblinking.

Lifeless.

TWENTY-SEVEN
THE END OF WAR?

A nthony stood over his father's grave, sweating in the blistering July sun. The tears flowed freely down his cheeks. It had been a full year since he had visited his father's grave.

As a boy, he had visited his father weekly. He had begged and pleaded with his mother to take him until it had become part of their weekly schedule. As Anthony got older, the frequency of their visits lessened. Not that Anthony didn't want to see his father. Quite the opposite actually. His father was a hero. And while the United States Government hadn't given him an honorable discharge because of the fight he had gotten into with an officer, Anthony's mother had fought tooth and nail to get him buried in a military cemetery.

Eventually, someone agreed. Simpson had saved many men overseas and had devoted his life back home to save wayward veterans. Anthony could think of no one more dedicated to the men and women who had served.

The reason Anthony stopped visiting his father, aside from on the Fourth of July holiday, was simple. The United States Military had taken too much from Anthony, and he couldn't stand to be around so many dead service members. Both Anthony's father and his uncle had lost their lives in service to their country.

His Uncle Xavier had died in some kind of classified operation in Iraq, and they had not declassified the details, even now. Hell, the body had never even been released. All they had was a gravestone. There was nobody in the casket.

His father hadn't died overseas, but he died trying to save a bunch of guys who had gone to war and given up so much of themselves overseas that when they came home, they were too fucked up to ever function properly again

Anthony wiped his eyes and clenched his fists. Someone had to pay for this, he was eighteen now, no longer a boy. He didn't know how he would avenge his father, but he knew he was going to make sure that something like this would never happen again.

ALSO BY JOHN LYNCH

Woe to Those Who Dwell on Earth

AFTERWORD

Much of this book, including scenarios that seem implausible, are based in fact. Name's have been changed, scenarios have been exaggerated, but you would be surprised by how much of the fiction is fact. If you thought to yourself, "Why would a truck with no armor and no weapon, with holes rusted in the bottom be driving along IED infested roads", just know that I asked myself that same question when I actually drove that truck. It happens.

The idea for this book started with my short story "Collateral Damage" first published by Cemetery Gates Media.

The opening scene was an exact replication of my first experience with sleep paralysis, and for years I really believed that something was haunting me. Ray, while named after one of my best buddies from the Corps, is not based on anyone I know. Marcus is mashup of two of my buddies from the Corps.

After the story was published, I wanted to know what happened to Ray. Originally, the ghost haunting Ray was real, and I saw this book as a body hopping slasher, like Jason goes to hell but with a bunch of combat veterans. That didn't work, and it sucked, so I abandoned the project and spent the next two years writing short fiction and selling it to various markets.

It wasn't until I discovered "The Written in Red Podcast", which is hosted by Aron Beauregard, Daniel J. Volpe, Rowland Bercy Jr., and Carver Pike, that I decided I wanted to try my hand at writing a novel again. From May through September of 2022 I wrote the book you now hold in your hands. Thank you gentlemen, this book would not exist without your podcast.

When I revisited the book, I thought there was no possibility of salvaging it, so I scrapped the 25k word manuscript and rewrote it from the ground up. I expanded the opening scene and then thought to myself, *what if Ray snapped?* Unfortunately, that scenario has happened in real life, however, this is fiction and the last quarter or so of the book has zero basis in anything myself, or my brothers in arms have experienced.

What isn't fiction, and is absolutely based in reality, are the struggles that all of the characters in this book deal stemming from combat wounds, both mental and physical. Suicide has taken many men and women who managed to survive the various wars America has taken part in.

If you know a veteran who is struggling, or you yourself are that veteran, please know there is help. You aren't alone. You can contact the Veterans Crisis line by dialing 988, and then pressing 1.

If you, or someone you know is contemplating suicide, please you can also dial 988 and talk to someone. Nothing is worth taking your own life.

ACKNOWLEDGMENTS

Thank you, reader, for giving this book a chance. I hope you enjoyed your time at The Warrior Retreat.

ABOUT THE AUTHOR

John Lynch is a USMC veteran, and horror writer from Rhode Island. He lives with his wife, kids, cat, and English Bulldog.

Visit my shop for signed books and merch.

Sign up for my newsletter for cover reveals, discounts, news on appearances and upcoming projects.

Printed in Great Britain
by Amazon

38198934R00111